# CANCER

The Heart Filled Story of a Father's Love For His Son

# An Ocean
# of Tears

## Jack J. Laurie

**ENDEAVORS**
**Dayton, New Jersey**

# What they are saying about
## *Cancer: An Ocean of Tears*

"*Cancer: An Ocean of Tears*, is the moving account of a father courageously coming to terms with his son's grave illness and lovingly walking with his son through the transition of dying. Jack Laurie's account opens a window for us into the emotional and spiritual dynamics of illness and dying. As a trained family therapist and a clergy person I recommend his book as required reading for hospital staff and pastoral care givers. It gives us all a lot to think about."

*The Rev. Fred Schott, M. Div., Th. M.,*
*S. T. M. Pastor, Christ the King Church (ELCA)*

"The principles that are pursued in Ranger and Special Forces training were imparted from father to son at a time when strength and courage of mind and spirit was most demanded. This story isn't about who is the most physically strong—it is about the mental toughness and attitude that determines who we are and how we deal with adversity. Joshua is representative of a hero who will live in our hearts forever and stand as an example of bravery—the likes of which we should all be proud."

*Brigadier General (R) Frank J. Toney, Jr.,*
*Former Commanding General,*
*United States Army Special Forces Command*

"Jack Laurie shares his heart filled story of his feelings and relationship with his son during one of life's most crushing blows. At times I found myself laughing out loud while at other times I shed a parent's tears. To understand a parent's love every child should read this. This book touches the reader at a place only shared with a few."

*Carol A. Kivler,*
*author of "Blessings," speaker, and trainer*

"I picked up *Cancer: An Ocean of Tears* one evening and literally never stopped reading until I finished it. This book is an incredible tribute to Joshua Laurie written not with a pen, but rather with his father's heart. It is an insightful book for all parents coping with their child's cancer diagnosis. It is not just a story about life and death. We take a journey with a father and son and their meaningful look at living and loving, and dying with dignity."

*Barbara Kessler,*
*Medical Office Manager*

"Jack Laurie writes with such care and tenderness that at times it is hard to remember that as a former Green Beret he is one of our countries most elite fighting men. It has been said no man is stronger than when he reaches down to help another, Jack's book proves that this is the case. It also shows that no matter the training one receives life will give you challenges that truly test your soul. Jack's spirit shines through."

*Dr. William Horton,*
*author of "Gorilla NLP"*

"Little did Jack know when he named his son after a biblical figure identified as a 'savior' and 'deliverer' how prophetic his choice would become. Just as Joshua led the Israelites into the Promised Land, Jack leads us on his personal journey coping with the untimely passing of his son. Hopefully, as a result, others experiencing similar unfortunate circumstances will take solace and comfort that they are not alone in their own travails."

*Mark Tobias,*
*Committeeman, Washington Township, NJ*

# More of what they are saying about *Cancer: An Ocean of Tears*

"As a pediatric oncologist, I recognize that most of my relationship with a child and the family is built upon an endless number of encounters in both the clinic and in the hospital. Although such a relationship may be both intimate and emotional, it remains one of remarkably brief interactions focused on fixing day to day complications and on the goal of achieving remission and cure. But what happens after the physician leaves the room or when the family goes home? How does a family cope with fighting off life-threatening illness with medicines, which sometimes seem worse than the disease? Reading *Cancer: An Ocean of Tears* provides a sometimes eye-opening exposure to what the doctor rarely sees—how deeply the diagnosis of leukemia impacts upon not only the child and the family, but also all aspects of life."

*Dr. Lisa A. Michaels,*
*M.D. Associate Professor of Pediatrics,*
*Pediatric Hematology and Oncology, Member,*
*Cancer Institute of New Jersey*

"Jack has given us a real insight into the journey some of us must take and the lessons we must learn from the death of a child through illness. His style is open, clear and entertaining and his message is timely and touching. I have never lost a child to death but Jack made me feel as though I was an integral part of his story and his learning."

*Tim Connor, CSP,*
*best selling author, speaker and trainer*

"A compelling journal of a father's journey to come to terms with the passing of his son and the lessons he learned. Your heartstrings are tugged as you find yourself emotionally engaged, holding back tears at times. A heartfelt experience any parent can relate to."

*Stephanie L. Labanowski,*
*Town Councilor, State of Connecticut*

"This remarkable story will hold your attention from beginning to end. Writing honestly and vividly, Jack Laurie reveals the hopes, the fears, and the heroic struggle of an exceptional father and a courageous son. You will always remember *Cancer: An Ocean of Tears.*"

*John Fludas,*
*Professor of English, Union County College*

"Through the eyes of a parent, the reader experiences a very candid and personal account of one family's endeavors to help their child experience life to the fullest with the time given to them. It tugs at the human heart strings!"

*Doreen Carnvale,*
*Pediatric RN, M.S.N., College Instructor*

"Jack Laurie writes this book, about his son Joshua, in a manner that is emotionally moving, sad, and funny at times. He talks about smoking cigars with Joshua, sleeping under the bed, and even sneaking into movies. What he did is to treat Joshua, although a teenager, as a complete adult, friend, and loved one. Jack made me cry especially during Joshua's last moments on earth. I will not easily forget this story about a courageous young man and a father, and the rest of the family and friends, who stood by him right to the end."

*Jerry Valley,*
*author of "Stage Hypnosis"*

# CANCER
# AN OCEAN OF TEARS

## Copyright © 2004

Printed in the United States

Library of Congress Cataloging-in-Publication Data
LCCN:   2004091021
Author:   Laurie, Jack J.
Title:   Cancer: An Ocean Of Tears
Editors:   John Fludas and Carol Mulligan
ISBN:   0-9748369-8-2

Cover photo – Brad Perks
Cover Design – Jim Weems
Text design – Barb Weems

Any questions, comments, or observations may be e-mailed to **Jackjlaurie@aol.com**. If e-mailing place the words: Comment – Ocean of Tears, in the subject line; please. We welcome all visitors to our web sites at www.canceranoceanoftears.com and www.jacklaurie.com. **All** comments and observations can remain private if desired.

## HAVE A STORY?

After you have read *Cancer: An Ocean of Tears*, visit www.canceranoceanoftears.com and send us your story. Let the world celebrate your friend or family member's life. Sharing helps the healing. Take it from one who knows. Cancer survivor stories happily accepted as well. *Jack J. Laurie, M.S.A., author*

## Need a speaker? See "About the Author" at book's end.

# DEDICATION

To Pat, Kristin, Dakota, Iliana and any, and all little
smiles that might appear in the future.

# IN MEMORY

Rest in Peace SFC Earl Fillmore Jr.
The man with the little boy smile
who went behind the big green fence.

# TABLE OF CONTENTS

# FOREWORD

There are some things I should point out as you're reading this book. I had toyed with the idea of actually researching everything I was going to write about. Then I decided this was not going to be about my experiences as a doctor or as a researcher. This is my experience as just plain old me, just Jack, the parent. So as you read this, you're not going to see a bunch of names of drugs. You're not going to see much of protocol guidelines. You're not going to see a step-by-step approach on how Joshua went through his treatment for his leukemia. What you're going to read is how different things affected me during his treatment, and how the different people reacted to aspects of his treatment. This writing is probably pretty selfish. I wanted to write it and I did. So if your child is sick and you're looking for some guidance as to what the treatment should be, don't use this book because Joshua's treatment would be and is totally different from what your child's would be. Of course, I also thought in the back of my mind, that maybe, just maybe, my story could help at least one other person get through the hard times, and perhaps appreciate the good times. Since the end of Joshua's treatment, the protocols have already changed. The drugs have changed. The parameters of which they treat different aspects of the disease have changed. So don't use this writing in any way to determine what you should or shouldn't do for your own child. This is just about one child. My child and his journey.

# CHAPTER I

# The Beginning

Friday morning started out like any other morning that starts out in a hospital room. I guess it was about 11:00 a.m. when the medical staff said they were ready for my wife and I in the conference room. **The Room**. Everyone has his or her own memories of **The Room**. The medical staff walks you in and asks you to take a seat. My wife and I sat on the right side of the long conference table. I was closer to the door than she was. It has been suggested that I took this seated position because on a subconscious level I felt the need to escape from the situation that we were about to be involved with. Pat, my wife, sat directly to my right and in a position further in as you entered the room. At the head of the table sat the doctor in charge. Directly across from him at the other end of the table were more doctors and social workers. Across from us were three or four medical students, same number of nurses, and other support people whom we would get to know very well in the future. The doctor at the head of the table carried a heavy binder. This binder contained all the various protocols that patients follow in their treatment.

For what seems like forever, you sit there with eyes glued to the surroundings as the players get set. As they fidgeted about, we sat there hoping they would get things started. With a clinic named "Pediatric Hematology & Oncology," things are not going to get better just yet. The silence is deafening. Finally, after the suspense began to feel like it was suffocating me, the doctor looks over and says the words "leukemia; your child has cancer."

So how did this journey begin? I had toyed with the idea that I would try to hide the sex of the child as if I were some really great mystery writer. Then I thought that's real silly. Parents hope for a boy or a girl when their kids are still in mommy's tummy. Truth is that after the little tyke comes out, the only thing that you care about is that he or she has ten fingers and ten toes. All the other hopes and desires melt into the little miracle's smile. My child just happened to be a thirteen-year-old boy named Joshua.

In the summer Joshua's neck swelled up. He actually looked like a bullfrog. We originally took him to the doctor and saw his substitute, his fill-in, his on-call person, if you will. The substitute doctor made the casual observation that it was probably a reaction to either allergies or the mononucleosis that he had previously that year. Either way, it was probably not that big a deal. She did make the mention that there was only the very, very slim chance that there was some kind of cancer related things. My wife put the idea of cancer in the back of her mind because of the way the on-call doctor expressed the notion. His neck stayed swelled. He had no trouble breathing. There were no other indications that he had a problem other than the fact that his neck was swollen. We had booked a cruise, and just prior to leaving, this swelling was still a concern. We took him back to the doctor. He checked everything out and said going on the cruise would be perfectly fine, but that he would set Joshua up to see an allergist. Subsequent to that, we went on the cruise, taking not only Joshua but his friend Ernie as well. Taking Ernie was a great way to provide a great trip for everyone. The fun he and Joshua had outweighed the expense of taking Ernie. Since they were off in their own little world, my wife and I had the opportunity to have fun too. The cruise lasted four days. The swelling was still there, and it still wasn't bothering him. By the time the trip ended and I had been home a few days, I was getting miffed with the whole "neck swelling thing." My wife called his pediatrician and said that we really needed to do something. I was getting irritated with the fact that nothing was being done, even though there was no outward sign that this was a problem. We expressed to the doctor that we did have an appointment with the allergist, but it was six to seven weeks away and this is just something we needed to take care of. His response was that he would make a phone call and call us back. It wasn't too long before he called us back and said they moved the appointment up to later that afternoon. Pat took Joshua down to see the allergist. At this point everyone believed that his condition was still allergy related. As Joshua walked into the doctor's office, the allergist took one look at him and determined that he should have blood work and a chest x-ray done. It was unusual that instead of sending us to the lab, he sent us to the hospital to have the blood work done. He stated he had suspicions and needed a few tests run. We had the tests performed on Tuesday.

Later that Tuesday afternoon Pat was approached by the x-ray technician and was told that the doctor would be calling soon to explain the test results. What was remembered most about the conversation was the uneasiness in the technician's voice as she spoke to my wife. It wasn't long after Pat arrived home that the doctor called and stated that the test indicated there might be problems. We didn't know at the time, but it was the chest x-ray that set things in motion. The doctor wanted us to have further tests performed at Robert Wood Johnson Hospital, and to do them Joshua would need to be admitted overnight. At this time, I still did not think anything was too bad.

That night Pat had to watch our daughter Kristin's little boy Koty, so I, with my son in tow, arrived at the hospital at about 5:00 p.m. I was told to bring him to the children's ward called "PEDIMOCK." At the time I did not give the acronym much thought. We entered through the emergency room and asked the security guard sitting at the desk how we could get to "PEDIMOCK." He looked at us funny. After a few moments, he asked if we meant Ped-Hem-Oc. I stated I guess so, and he waived us to follow him. So the two of us, like little ducks, just followed the guard through the emergency room and out the back entrance. At this time I still did not think that these tests were much to do about anything.

There are certain things one never forgets. When I was in the Army, I attended Ranger School. Anyone who has ever attended that particular school and graduated will always remember his class number. My class number was 1-74. I can tell you now that the first time you realize something is bad concerning your child, that moment will be etched in your mind permanently. I liken it to the way a branding iron burns into the hide of an unsuspecting animal. We followed the guard around the corner and down a long hallway. He stopped, turned around, acted very professional, and then pointed to the sign ahead. I will never forget reading that sign for the first time. It hung approximately 6 inches down from the ceiling. It was not a very impressive sign; just your standard, simple hospital sign pointing you in the right direction. It read: **PEDIATRIC HEMATOLOGY AND ONCOLOGY**.

I knew the hematology part had to do with blood. It was the oncology part that my brain just could not process. I felt my brain shifting through years of experience, trying to remember the other word for oncology. My medical background told me that oncology was the fancy word for cancer. As I stated before there are many moments in a person's life that one never forgets. We remember our first kiss, our first love, the first time we buy a car, the day we get married, and the day our children were born. I can say with the utmost certainty, the first time you look up and see that sign is a moment you will never forget.

I signed Joshua in Tuesday night. The rooms were actually quite nice. The rooms were divided; some rooms held two people, others were singles. We would learn later that the first time you get admitted, they always put you in a single room. At the end of the clinic was a rather large single room for holding patients that can only have limited contact with others. There was also a large room for meetings and such. That was the room that we would soon refer to only as, **The Room**. There was also a small room with a refrigerator, ice machine, and cabinets where snacks and things were stored. Facing all the rooms was the nursing station where assistance could always be found. Behind the station in a little storage room was where they kept towels and blankets and the various medical things with which we would become very familiar.

### Wednesday

On Wednesday the doctors ran some more tests. At this point in time, nobody had used the word "cancer" or any other diagnostic word around us. The doctors did tell us there were suspicions. But that so far, no one was sharing anything with us. Later that day we got back the test results. Still no "C" word yet. One more test needed to be performed before we were told. The final test, for this sequence would be to take a bone marrow sample from Joshua's hip. This test would create what medical types refer to as definitive diagnoses. The results would tell conclusively with what we were dealing.

## Thursday

The biopsy surgery took place today. Briefly, the surgery consisted of a procedure that required the patient to be under general anesthesia. Once under, a large needle was used to extract bone marrow from the patient's hipbone. The bone marrow samples were tested with results creating a definitive piece of proof as to what we would be dealing with. The procedure was done in the morning. We were told that everything went well and that the results would be ready the next day. Still no one was taking a guess as to what my son was dealing with. When Joshua had his first biopsy, we noticed a guy in a suit looking at his chart. We wondered who he was because we had not noticed him before. We didn't think he was a doctor. So the first person we saw that we did recognize was asked, "Who is he?" The response was simple: "He is the guy from the insurance company." Didn't take them long to get on board. Our insurance was PHS, now called Healthnet. If you need an insurance recommendation, they have mine. All Joshua's treatments were covered.

One funny thing about insurance, depending on your state, is that of continuous coverage. Hypothetically speaking, did you know that if you have really lousy insurance when you get diagnosed, you "might" be able to switch to a premium policy that will cover everything without having to worry about the "previous illness clause?" One more interesting fact about life insurance policies is that in some states if you get life insurance and pay into the policy for two years, then no matter what, the policy will be in effect. This may also be true even if you might have forgotten to include "all" medical information. This is something to contemplate since a person with cancer may not be insurable later on in life.

### Friday

This was the day we were to find out what was going on. So far numerous doctors, a collection of students, and several nurses who by all accounts were really nice, but were still not giving any answers, had seen Joshua. Friday morning started out like any other morning that starts out in a hospital room; quiet. I guess it was about 11:00 a.m. when they said they were ready for us in the conference room, **The Room.**

As stated before, **The Room** experience is unique, but shared by all the parents on this particular hospital ward. I think the hardest thing I ever did in my entire life was to just sit there and stay calm. Everyone watches the movie of the week on TV. Sure, we have seen the movies about the kids, the wives, and the friends who have cancer. We feel bad for the person, or actor, then we go on to another show. Until the reality of it hits you, you will never understand its impact. We hear it, we listen to the words, and most of us even understand the dialog. But I can tell you now, until you are told that your loved one has cancer, you have no idea of the impact of that six-letter word.

So you sit there. Soon the doctor starts reading all the different propaganda he is supposed to tell you. You listen, you take mental notes, and you try to remain calm as much as possible. After what seems like forever, but in reality is a matter of minutes, you ask the only question that comes to mind, "Will he live?"

# CHAPTER II

# Learning the Answer

Learning the answer to that single question is the ultimate test in patience. The doctor told us that under the current treatment, there is a success rate of 95 percent. At this point I was just trying to maintain my composure. To tell you the truth, in matters such as these, my wife is much stronger than I am. I don't even know how she does it. I started to cry before the doctor finished the word "leukemia."

My tears caused the doctor to stop his oration. I remember with tears flowing, winding my finger in a circular motion, so the doctor would keep talking. Interrupting the session because of a father's tears made no sense. We needed the information and I knew myself well enough to know that I was not going to stop crying.

They told us our options. They told us what the next few years would most likely bring. One of the biggest hurdles we had to overcome immediately was the need to find out if the leukemia cells were present in the spinal fluid. Unfortunately it would be a few days before we would know the result of that test.

So armed with this new information, my wife and I retreated to the hallway into each other's arms. I had just about gotten my breath back when the doctor walked up to us and asked us to return to the conference room. I was not sure what was going on when all of a sudden all the same people who were in the room before marched back in with us. Now this is something you have to picture in your mind. You walk into **The Room**, with 20 other people following and the doctor looks at you and says he has to apologize. He carries the conversation further because in his words, he made a mistake. A mistake, what kind of mistake?

He looked at us and said he was looking at the wrong protocol. He had made a mistake of thinking Joshua was 10 years old and had just realized he was 13. I asked, "So?" I remember him looking very sheepish. He looked at my wife and said he had made a mistake on the survival rate. Joshua had already entered puberty. He had explained about the survival rate of a child who had not entered puberty yet. The survival rate for children 10 years and younger was as high as 95 percent but Joshua was older than 10. I remember looking at him. I'm not sure what I was feeling but the obvious question was what impact was Joshua's age going to have on his survival rate. He looked sad, and before he said anything, he apologized again for the mistake, and then told us the survival rate was only as high as 75 percent.

I remember how I felt at that point. I pictured myself in a high school gym class with a hundred children lined up against the bleachers. The bleachers were all folded up against the wall. The gym teacher was calling out the names of five kids and asking them to cross to the other side of the gym. He tells the rest of the class to hit the showers. The five kids sent over, they are dead. Five was not a large number. Those are good odds. Now I pictured, as other students are leaving the gym, they stop when the coach blows his whistle. Everyone looks back and hears him yell to line up again. He then takes 20 more students and pulls them to the other side of the gym. Five did not seem like a large group; 25 did. I know it was selfish of me to think that my son would not be part of the five. I could handle the odds of 5 out of 100. Now I had to go explain to my son that his odds of living were 75 out of 100. I felt bad for the doctor; he felt humiliated about making the mistake.

So, we stayed in the conference room for a while. We pretty much asked the same questions again. Looking back, I remember that one of the other doctors had said she did not like to discuss odds with parents because the bottom line was, if your child survived, the survival rate was a hundred percent. If your child died, the survival rate was zero.

A decision had to be made on the spot concerning future children for Joshua. The chemotherapy (chemo) that he would have to start would certainly destroy any chance of him fathering children. The doctor's concern was that the labs in the area that dealt with storing sperm would be closed until Tuesday because of the Labor Day holiday. The doctor running the meeting felt that waiting five more days to start the chemo was not a smart thing. The decision on our part was simple. Lets deal with keeping him alive today. We will worry about tomorrow when it gets here.

The next big step was to tell Joshua. I'm not sure why, but I knew that was going to have to come from me. I had no idea how I was going to tell him. They gave us some books that we could let Joshua read. I did not see that happening; Joshua did not like to read. I also knew that this was one time that I would not be allowed to cry. You have to understand, my kids have seen me cry on many occasions. I cry when I get presents, I cry when I get emotional. Hell, I cried every time I saw *Beauty and the Beast* on Broadway. Joshua needed to know that this was just one of life's little hurdles and that this too shall pass.

Before I entered the room, I had already made one major decision. What Joshua was going to need over the next few years was a father. He was not going to need another friend or pal, or someone that he could unwind with. Joshua was going to need someone that he could hold on to and that would not tell him everything was all right when it wasn't. What he was going to need now more than ever was a dad! I entered the room they had assigned him. He was just lying there in bed waiting for some news of any kind. He already knew things were not going to be pleasant. I don't remember how I told him. I am not even sure of the words I used. I do remember his reaction. He just sat there and looked at me. The doctors told us he was in denial. I didn't think so. I believe that he just didn't figure he knew what to say just yet. As time went on, I came to find out that I was right.

# CHAPTER III

# The Treatment Starts

Different things happened along the way in Joshua's treatment. Among the things I remember mostly was his attitude. He had a very good attitude. Very standoffish to most people, but a very good attitude as far as I was concerned. One of the things we discussed when he was doing the chemo was wasted energy. I wasn't sure how he was going to accept what I was going to tell him, but I sat him down anyway. I told him that one of the things we learned in Ranger School was that complaining about something served no purpose. It was wasted energy and it was counterproductive. Not wasting energy became a real important thing to him. A lot of the times when he was on chemo, it made him sick, and some days were just bad days. It was interesting how well Joshua held things together for a thirteen-year-old young man. Joshua would express his condition using statements similar to, "I really feel like shit today." I would look at him and say, "Okay, I understand." Then for the rest of the day, he would never bring it up again. He wouldn't bring it up again unless things got really bad. Now that's not to say that we didn't treat what was causing him the discomfort. He would say, "I feel nauseous" and we would give him the various medications for that. He would have a headache and we gave him medications for that. Whatever was bothering him, he would discuss it but he would discuss it in a very calm manner and not in a complaining whine. This went on for his entire treatment. I was very impressed with him.

I've seen adults going through various forms of military training where they get a little cold, wet, and miserable, they become crybabies and argumentative and they just get to the point that they won't cooperate and they actually no longer function. In Special Forces (better known as U.S. Army Green Berets) training, we would see this a lot. Unfortunately, those who could not get their act together were dropped from training. The mechanism for dropping those individuals having difficulties was either instructor's or peer reports. In Ranger School it was even harder; if you so much as raised your voice, they would give you minus points. Minus points could cause you to be thrown out, or worse; recycled (forced to start over). For a thirteen-year-old to have the ability to acknowledge he doesn't feel well, acknowledge the fact that you have accepted what he said, and then to drop it and get on with the day was a very impressive thing for me as a parent.

Every time Joshua went into the hospital, he took advantage of his stay to watch videos. He would request certain movies of the local video store and a gentleman named Toby would see to it that he had a good selection to peruse. Toby proved to be a great ally in the fight against the boredom of hospital stays. The local video store became a very good source of enjoyment for Joshua. They would not give us a hard time about maybe getting the movies back a little bit late. Additionally, if a new release came out, the video staff would get the movie to him a day or two before the general public was allowed to view the tape. These early viewings were a highlight, almost a perk when he was in the hospital.

When he first got in the hospital, he and I would have discussions. His denial of his illness was not really that; it was nothing more than he had not gotten to the point where he wanted to talk about it. I accepted that. I did push a little bit in the beginning that this is what you have. This is cancer. I told Joshua that there are going to be treatments he's going to have. He had to understand that certain phases of the treatment were really going to "suck." The premise that this is going to hurt me more than it hurts you is total bullshit and the fact is that it was going to hurt him more than it was going to hurt me. When I told him that, his response was "No shit." We had various understandings right from the get-go.

The first thing I promised Joshua was that he would never be in the hospital overnight by himself. In all his hospital stays, this would become very, very important. Many of the teenagers up there spent many nights alone. Many smaller children remained alone as well. I always felt bad for these kids. I understood that some family circumstances would not allow for a parent or guardian to remain all night. Some kids came from single parent homes with other siblings, while others were from outside the area making it impossible to remain on the ward, and still get to work. I'm not sure why I thought it was important that he never be alone at night, but it just was. For me, it seemed like it was my duty to be by my son's side. Logistically, it just worked out better for me to stay nights at the hospital. Pat was the keeper of the household and also was providing some assistance to Kristin as a young mom for the first time. We had a business to run and Pat was involved in that heavily. The business was a radon company and Pat processed all the orders in the morning to be shipped out to all the various engineering companies. That's not to say that she wasn't at the hospital every day during the afternoon. She actually got the worst of the duties as far as I'm concerned. Pat had a routine that couldn't be altered whereas mine had some degree of flexibility. All I had to do was show up at the hospital by seven or eight o'clock at night, sit there, eat a little bit, talk to Joshua, maybe watch TV, and then go to sleep. To me, I always looked at it like I was deployed (sent off on military assignment). I never knew when I would be going home and I just had to face the fact that I was away from home and there was nothing I could do about it.

The hospital had these little blue chairs that when you pulled out the bottom, the top would fall back and essentially what it did was make a little twenty-four-inch-wide bed. If you ever find yourself in this position, fixing the chair for sleep is easy. First you pull the lower ledge out and lay the back down. The chair is now in the prone position. Take a heavy quilt and lay it on the chair. Now you add one air mattress. I got mine at K-Mart. If you do buy an air mattress, buy the larger pump. It makes life a lot easier when you inflate the air mattress. Then you put another quilt-type blanket on top of the air mattress and then a sheet and you lay on the sheet. It actually makes a very comfortable bed. Well, that's probably an exaggeration, but it does make a bed.

Joshua's big thing, I came to find out, was he didn't really like to talk until after midnight. There's something about talking before midnight that he just didn't do. So after midnight we talked about everything from his illness, to people, to death and dying. One thing I was impressed with was that he understood that leukemia could kill you. He had to come to terms with that possibility. It was during one of these initial conversations that I told him if it did come to pass that he was to die, that I would see to it that he did not die alone. It would be me who would hold him until he left us and that he was not to be afraid that he would be by himself at the end.

When it came time to talk with his doctors, I explained to him that it was his right. More important, it was his obligation to ask questions when he didn't understand something. I'm not sure at what age an individual should start to control his own path. All I did know was that Joshua was going to be guided, but that he also would have a say in his treatment. I made it clear to him that if he had guests in the room and he needed to talk to his doctor, he was to tell the guests politely to step out of the room. My guidance here was to include myself as well. If he needed to talk to his doctor about his treatment or anything, and he felt that he would prefer privacy, then he was obliged to follow his desire. If he wanted privacy, it was his right to have it. I made no bones about it. No one was to be spared being removed from the room should he wish it. This was not limited to any particular guests or me. Having the ability to ask others to leave was all encompassing, to include but not limited to his mother, his sister, my parents or anybody else. I also made sure that this mandate included any nurses or staff personnel that he might not want in the room during these discussions. During the treatments that he went through, he availed himself of this to include asking me to step out of the room. No discussion was ever made; nobody was to ever ask him why he or she couldn't stay. I gave explicit instructions to everybody that if Joshua asked them to leave the room, there would be no discussion and to just vacate the room.

I remember the first time Joshua asked me to leave the room so he could talk with his doctor. I left the room and waited outside by the main nursing station. They were in there for ten to fifteen minutes and then his doctor came out. I inquired about what they had discussed. She said she wasn't sure if she should discuss what he had said in private to her with me. My response to her was that as far as your relationship with him, anytime he wants to talk to you, you're free to talk to him about anything and everything in his treatment and that I would make sure that he didn't know I was part of the loop. But anything that he asked her or discussed with her, she was to immediately tell me about and that I would keep her confidence and I wouldn't relay anything to him unless it became so serious that I felt I had to violate his trust. As it was during his entire treatment, that never came to pass. But anytime his doctors talked to him privately, they would tell me what was discussed. I was kept abreast of all his questions, his state of mind, and any and all concerns that he might have. This gave him a feeling of control regarding his own destiny and progress through his treatments.

It became obvious pretty quickly that the chemo he was going to take was not going to make his day; it was not going to be a happy experience. I'm not going to turn this into a manual, but one thing we found out that worked really, really well with Joshua when he was undergoing chemo was keeping him hydrated and using the drug Zofran. Every time he would have his chemo, we would literally run three 1000 milliliter bags of IV fluid through him to keep him extremely hydrated and that made things work rather well.

One of the things that came up rather quickly was the possibility that this illness could actually be terminal. Joshua handled that pretty well. I think he had an understanding of it. He and I had numerous discussions on that possibility right from day one; well, maybe day two. I had already promised Joshua that he would never spend the night alone in the hospital, that became very important to him. I came to find out that he never got nervous about me being in the hospital until about seven or eight o'clock at night. He would start asking, "Where's Daddy? Is Daddy coming tonight?" He would start getting nervous around eight o'clock as to whether I was coming and lo and behold, even if I got there late, he came to realize that no matter how late it got, I was coming to the hospital. He never asked me not to come. Occasionally, we would get into an argument and he would make the comment to the effect that nobody asked you to come. But he would never go so far as to say, "You don't need to come." I never pushed it. What was interesting is that in all his machismo and all his self-assurance, one action gave him away that he was still a little boy at times. I'd be laying there in my little corner of the room, when out of the corner of my eye, late at night, I would see him sit up, look over, and make sure I was still there. After he would see me, he would turn over and go back to sleep. It was those little glances that totally convinced me I made the right decision by being there every night.

There were times that I went out of town that couldn't be helped. During these times his sister filled in and stayed there at night. It didn't happen often that I couldn't be at the hospital with him. When it did, Kristin was always ready to step in.

The initial treatment he underwent was some really strong chemo. The swelling on his neck almost immediately disappeared. Robert Wood Johnson is a teaching hospital. As such, there would be a lot of students to come along and poke him and prod him. For the most part, he put up with that during his hospital stays. He didn't particularly like it. He would quiz the medical students to make sure they knew what they were talking about. He got a kick out of grilling them, more so if they didn't know the answer. He enjoyed giving the nurses a hard time as well. Another thing he liked to do was negotiate. During one of his stays in the clinic, he had to give a urine sample. He didn't feel like doing it, so he charged the doctor two dollars for the sample. The doctors were pretty neat when it came to dealing with kids. One of the doctors actually paid him two dollars for a urine sample. We would come to find that the initial stay in the hospital was probably going to go 35 to 40 days at a minimum, and it pretty much did that. If you deal with leukemia, you're going to spend time in the hospital. Any time they admit you, you're looking at ten days minimum. I don't care if they're admitting you because they're concerned about a hangnail or because you have a high temperature. Understand that when you go back into the hospital, you're going to be there for ten days. Joshua and the rest of the family quickly realized that asking when you could go home was wasted energy. Essentially when you were hospitalized, you figured you'd be in there as long as needed and you weren't leaving until they were sure you could go home.

(Special Note: Hospitals and protocols differ on the number of days a child will spend in the hospital given their condition. Some hospitals/protocols allow for shorter stays. The above was our experience.)

Most diseases have a pattern they follow. Likewise their treatment has certain milestones that must be met. With leukemia there are three milestones that must be overcome. The first obstacle we faced after diagnosis was that there was a great hope that there were no leukemia cells in the spinal fluid. We received the news on the Monday after the original biopsy. I remembered I was standing at the nursing station when one of the doctors looked up and said that the spinal fluid was clean; there was no trace of leukemia cells in the spinal fluid. I remembered immediately tearing up and all I could say was, "I knew that would be the case" while trying to hold back tears. Holding back tears-what an interesting concept. When your child gets sick, that is the first ability that will go by the wayside.

The next hurdle comes at day 14. On day 14 the chemo should have the leukemia cells down to less than 25%. Joshua's came in at around 23%. To say we were happy would be a gross understatement. Next hurdle comes at day 28; cells need to be fewer than 5%. Joshua's blood was clean. Joshua was now in remission. Remission is a concept that most do not understand. Getting someone into remission is not the problem; keeping them there is. After the initial onslaught of the chemo, the maintenance chemo is to keep the patient in remission. The game plan at this point was to watch and wait.

Every time Joshua got admitted into the hospital, he always took full advantage of videos and food. He would always ask for two or three movies to be brought up. His favorite eating-place would become Red Lobster. He enjoyed asking for us to bring him a fish dinner, a lobster or crab legs. He had other foods he liked, but the Red Lobster diet became his favorite. We kept him stocked with various things like applesauce and cookies. That was the nice thing about leukemia; even though he had leukemia, it really didn't matter what he ate. It wasn't like he had some restricted diet, so he could eat whatever he wanted. Whenever he was admitted for various hospital stays, if you opened one of the drawers in his room, one of the things you would always find was that it was packed with food. One really good source for food was grandparents. My mother has the recipe for biscuits that Red Lobster puts together and she makes them from scratch. Every time he went into the hospital, he would ask for these biscuits to be made. My mother didn't go to the hospital very often, so she sent the food to represent her. She was constantly sending these biscuits up with my father. Joshua liked pizza, too. He felt pizza was slumming it, but if he couldn't have lobster or shrimp, it would work. But he really liked Grandma's biscuits. The other thing he really liked was the pasta shells filled with cheese. He could lay a guilt trip on my mother so quick it was pathetic. "If you bring me some shells, that wouldn't be a bad thing," he would say. So we would call my mother and tell her that Joshua needed some more shells. Lo and behold, they would show up at the hospital within a day or two. My mom was constantly sending up the stuffed shells with my father.

The hospital itself had a little refrigerator, kitchen, and break area. The kitchen was always filled with cookies, cheese and crackers, milk, various juices, sodas, and ice cream.

# CHAPTER IV

# Hair, Cigars, and Biopsies

Hair is an interesting thing. I'm going to tell you the whole story about hair. When Joshua was a little over ten years old, he started letting his hair grow. I had never had long hair in my entire life. Between the military and other jobs that didn't allow for it—even in college I didn't have long hair. The longest my hair ever got was to the bottom of my ear, and that was it. Joshua's hair was now getting past his ear and in typical parental fashion, I told him he needed to cut his hair. Most likely the only reason that I told him to cut it was because when I was young my Dad told me to cut mine. In typical child response, he stated that he wasn't cutting his hair. This was the first time he took a stance and he was not going to waiver from it. So we're standing in the house and we're arguing to the point that I'm getting extremely loud and boisterous and threatening about him cutting his hair and he's standing his ground saying he's not going to cut his hair. As I'm yelling at him, I'm thinking I'm painting myself into a corner and the more I'm yelling, the darker the paint is getting and the smaller the corner is getting. I'm starting to think in conjunction with yelling at him that hair really isn't that big a deal. I've raised this child to be independent and self-thinking and self-motivating, and that is what he is doing, and now I'm giving him crap over it. So I'm trying to think how can I get out of this and still save face and still get my point across. So it was like a little light bulb went off and I said, "Fine, you don't want to cut your hair, that's great. You don't cut your hair, I don't cut my hair." He figured that was a joke. I told him, "No, you don't cut your hair, fine, I'm not cutting my hair." Now at the time it never dawned on me that some people's hair grows to a certain point and stops. I don't understand that process, but it's a truism. Over the years, his hair would grow to shoulder length and never extended past his shoulders. My hair, on the other hand, grew and grew and grew. At the point when he was admitted into the hospital, his hair was shoulder length. My hair was approximately two inches below my waist. So my hair had become longer than twenty-four inches or thereabouts and still growing. I called it my nine rubber bands because when I would go on my motorcycle, I would have to use nine rubber bands to keep it from getting all frayed and horrible and going every which way but loose.

So why do I bring this up? About his eighth month of treatment, he ended up losing his hair. It was really funny because what he did was molt like a bird and one night, he simply gave a little tug on his hair and it fell out in one piece. It was almost as if he had a wig on, and with one tug off it came. Well, this upset him. He was your typical fourteen-year-old and now he was almost bald and he had this peach fuzz for hair. As the typical parent, I told him, "Hair is not that big a deal. It'll grow back. Don't sweat the small stuff."

His reaction was typical of any teenager, "Easy for you to say, you have hair."

Well, after I left the hospital, the next morning I told my wife, "We're not wasting energy on this crap." So I went down to the barbershop and I told them to shave my head. That night when I showed up at the hospital, I thought he was going to pee in his pants because he was laughing so hard. He hadn't seen me with a shaved head at any point in his life. He had seen me with short hair because I had served my third tour in the military and he, his sister, and his mother were with me at Fort Bragg, North Carolina. There I had short hair, but nothing like what he was seeing now. He thought it was pretty comical that I went from hair over two feet long to no hair. As it would come to pass, every week or so I would shave my head. From that evening forward, nothing was ever said about hair again.

Each kid deals with the hair loss in his or her own way. Joshua never got into hats, so they were out. I had gotten these shirts from a very close friend in California named Cindy. They were for me but he took them over. The shirts were of a very thin, comfortable cloth. They were hooded much like a workout type sweatshirt. When he left the house, he would pull the hood up over his head. I told him it made him stand out more than the guy who was proverbially bald and grows his hair long in the back and flips it forward. He didn't seem to care. When he didn't have hair, the hooded shirt was what he wore. Nobody who mattered made any comments concerning the shirt.

As time went on, Joshua had more and more questions. Anytime Joshua had questions about things, I would tell him to go to his doctor or bring his doctor in and we would discuss it. I pounded it into him that if he had a question, he needed to ask and not sit on it. I further instructed him to make sure that if it wasn't answered to his satisfaction, whoever he was talking to should be made to stay there and answer it until he became comfortable with their response.

Another story I would like to share with you in order to give you a proper insight into Joshua. This particular incident took place the second time he was admitted to the hospital. It had only been a couple of weeks since he left the hospital after his initial stay. His second stay was just at the beginning of winter. That previous summer Joshua had made a big deal out of smoking something. He didn't care what; he just wanted to smoke. I never did find out why he had this great urge to consume a tobacco product. All I know was that our relationship was going to the dogs over it. So that summer I compromised. I let him have a cigar. The only thing about letting him have the cigar was that he really liked it. We had purchased a couple of cigars and took off to Great Adventure for a much-deserved break. This all happened before he was diagnosed with leukemia. This trip to Great Adventure is where he won the frog; more about that later. Why am I mentioning this now? Read on.

We were called into **The Room** with the doctors again to discuss some test results. "God, I came to hate **The Room**." As we sat there going over the last battery of tests and pondering Joshua's future, I stated that I had a question for them. I was motioned to ask away, and I looked at them and asked, "Will a cigar interfere with any of the drugs or chemo he is taking?" They looked at me and said that they were not going to advise me to give a thirteen-year-old a cigar. I gazed back and told them I wasn't asking them to, all I needed to know was would the cigar interfere with any of the medical protocols that he was following. Again, they stated that they were not going to advise a thirteen-year-old to have a cigar. This time I looked them right in the eye and stated very pointedly, "I didn't ask your permission to give it to him; I just need to know if it will interfere with his treatment, that's the question." Then one doctor looked at me and said "No, but" I stopped her there. "Thank you!"

That night I told Joshua we were going out onto the parking deck, it was a little after midnight. So I wrapped him up in a heavy winter coat, ski cap, and a scarf, and off we went. He was a sight. There he was in a heavy coat and all this other collateral stuff, pulling an IV pole with three pumps and at least 8 bags of IV fluids running into him. We set out to the parking deck facing French Street, New Brunswick, and there we stood with cigars in our hands. So as we were standing there I noticed Joshua flicking the ash off his cigar like it was a cigarette. I looked at him and I said, "The mark of a good cigar is that the tobacco burns even and the ash hangs at the end of the cigar." That is the reason that you see guys smoking cigars with inches of ash hanging on the end.

So he looks at me and starts to say, "Yea, but don't you know that they say...," and he starts laughing.

I looked at him and said, "Yea, and what's so funny?"

He looks back at me with a silly grin and says, "They tell you if you smoke through the ash, you have a better chance of getting cancer."

I looked over and just said, "Well, I guess that's a moot point."

"Yep" was his response, and we went on about smoking our cigars.

During his treatment, he had numerous biopsies. Biopsies are when they take a sample of tissue and analyze it. With

Joshua, most of the biopsies were from the bone marrow in his hip. Once Joshua made the comment that we didn't need to be there, and my response was we would always be there, and then it was never brought up again. Initially when he was diagnosed, my wife and I had the discussion that when he went in for these various biopsies, it would be her job because I would be at work. As it turned out, for whatever reason, every time he went in for surgery, we were both there and we both stayed there. Even if you make plans on how you're going to deal with certain things, as they come up, they're going to change.

For his biopsies, our routine was that we would both go into the pre-op room where they would prep him and make sure that his IVs were okay and ask all the questions, and then I would walk with him back to the operating room. They allowed the parents to go into the operating room. You stayed with the child until he or she was put under general anesthesia. Probably the hardest thing you'll ever do as a parent is walk your child into an operating room. Like sleeping in the hospital overnight, I figured this was my responsibility. I'm not sure how that came to be. Certain people in the family will take on certain responsibilities and it just seemed to work that way. The logistics of it seems to come about through no planning. It's just all of a sudden, this comes up and this is who deals with it. Initially I made the decision, which was probably arrogant, that the doctors would take care of the treatment, my wife would make sure he followed the treatment, and I would make sure he would have fun. I would let my wife take the brunt of, "You need to do this or else" kind of phase. Yet walking Joshua into the operating room became my responsibility. I did it every time.

What really made it easy was that Peggy was there. Peggy is the play therapist. It sounds kind of silly to have a play therapist. I came to find her to be extremely valuable. I nicknamed her Mighty Mouse®. Peggy is a short, little blonde. Somebody asked me if I thought she was attractive and I remember my response was, "I never really noticed." Peggy was Peggy. She was a fantastic person. She was also as important for Joshua's treatment as any of the doctors. She became extremely important to me when we went to surgery. You put on these sterile gowns and cap, and then you get masked up. What I would do is walk Joshua into the operating room and he would lie down on the surgical table and I'd be talking to him more or less. I would force myself to be very matter of fact. I had to give the impression that this was no big deal and let's get on with it. I would tell him that I would be waiting outside when he was done. It was portrayed as an everyday occurrence. Peggy would always stand at my side. Usually we'd be in the operating room together for four to six minutes and then they would put the mask on his face and he'd take a couple of deep breaths and they'd start medication going through his IV line and he would drift off to sleep. At that point, the Operating Room (OR) doctor would turn and say, "Okay, Dad, you can leave now." It seemed they always went out of their way to make me as comfortable as they did him.

Inevitably every time I would walk out of the OR into the corridor that led back into the waiting area, I would start to cry. Peggy would put her hand on my shoulder and her persona changed from that of a play therapist to a guard dog. Everybody would know to stay away from us and she would walk me out. She never talked. She never asked me if I was all right or if I needed anything. Essentially, she would just be there and keep everybody away from me. I liken it to being escorted by a pit bull. Everybody understands to stay away. Peggy and I went through numerous procedures and the end result was always the same.

Each time Joshua went into the Operating Room Peggy would walk me out and as soon as we cleared the door, I would immediately start crying. If I had cried going into the OR, it would simply make Joshua nervous, and that wouldn't be a good thing, so I held it inside until I knew he was asleep and I had left the OR. Peggy knew I would start crying. Hell, I knew I would start crying, so a routine was established.

There was one time when Peggy wasn't there. A different nurse walked me back to the OR and subsequently back out of the OR. The nurse who took her place was a very nice woman. As soon as I started crying, she asked me if I was all right, did I need a glass of water, did I need to sit down. I know she was trying to be helpful but I really missed Peggy.

It wasn't long after the first time Joshua went into the hospital to start his treatment that I had the opportunity to talk with my personal doctor. My doctor is the greatest doctor you could ever have. I could talk to him about anything, and he understood that when I got sick or injured, I needed to be treated quickly because I couldn't afford any downtime. I immediately conveyed to him that Joshua was sick and explained briefly what was going on in my life. I felt it was important to tell him because he was my doctor. One of the things he told me right off the bat was that if things started getting too hard emotionally, there were various medications available that I could use. My personal opinion and what I conveyed to him is that I appreciate his candor and his ability to do this, but I chose not to take them.

The biggest reason I chose not to take any kind of anti-depressant is because I had seen a friend of mine on them and witnessed what they did. Basically the antidepressants make the real bad times not real bad. Now the other side of that coin is, of course, that antidepressants make the really good times not real good. I realized we were going to have ups and downs over the next few years. That reality was a given. But if I took the medication, while certainly it wouldn't make me feel as bad during the down times, it would take away from the really good times that were sure to follow intermittently. So I made the decision never to take anything, even though the bad times were really bad. I always fell back on the fact that I made the right decision because the good times were really good. You should not infer by any means my course is the only course of action you should take. As I stated in the beginning, this book is not meant to be a guide on how you should or should not approach the treatment of your child. It's just my experiences. My experience with antidepressants was that they evened everything out, which wouldn't allow me to enjoy the good times. It created a level playing field for all experiences.

When dealing with leukemia, one of the things you have to watch out for is fever. Fevers indicate an infection. An infection is a serious thing when you're talking about people with suppressed immune systems. You always have to watch out for fevers. You call the hospital and tell them the child has a fever and they tell you bring the child to the hospital. The doctors conveyed to us that if we had a suspicion that something was wrong, we were to share it with them. When it came to the pediatric doctors, we found out that the doctors really listen to the parents. Parents are with the child 24/7. The little changes in the patient were noticed by the parents and were not always noted by the medical staff. This became real important on one of Joshua's emergency room visits. That's another thing you get used to: going into the emergency room. The nice thing about Robert Wood Johnson, with the Pediatric-Hematology-Oncology unit right there is that there's always an oncologist on call. When it came to the cancer kids, we never had a long wait in the Emergency Room (ER). We never waited long for a doctor. By the time you got there, the ER staff was already waiting for you. The most serious time we went through the Emergency Room (not to dismiss that any trips to the ER were petty) was about a year into his treatment.

# CHAPTER V

# ICU

P rior to this one particular visit to the ER, we were at home and Joshua called me to his bedroom. His voice had a ring of concern. His bedroom was at the left rear of the house. When I walked back there, I asked him what was the problem, and he said, "Look at this." He picked up the remote control of the TV but as he picked it up, it dropped out of his hand. I looked at him with a little smile and said, "Well, that's interesting. No big deal but just for the heck of it, I'll call the clinic." I've got some medical background. I was an EMT, and one of my last assignments in the 5th Special Forces Group was that of Battalion Medical NonCommissioned Officer. So I had a good idea of all the things that could be causing what I was seeing. The biggest concern I had was the possibility of a stroke. The effects of a stroke can be losing motor control or numbness in the extremities. I called the clinic and within a matter of minutes the oncologist doctor on call called me back. I told him that Joshua had numbness and lack of motor control in his hands. His response was what I anticipated. I was told to immediately bring him to the emergency room. One of their concerns was that he had had a stroke. The chemo drugs can do that. I got Joshua ready. We took off in the car.

We made the trip rather quickly. Point being we didn't play around. When I got him to the hospital, I didn't want to alarm Joshua so when I approached the triage nurse I simply said my son was a patient in the cancer clinic and we have a fourteen-year-old ALL (acute lymphocytic leukemia) patient with a possible CVA. Joshua didn't really know what CVA meant. For those of you that are non-medical types, Cardiovascular Accident, is another way of telling the nurse that I have a leukemia patient with a possible stroke. The ER staff didn't do a work-up or anything at the waiting desk. The ER nurse immediately took him, started an IV, proceeded to watch him, and called a neurologist. While we were in the emergency room, the ER staff put us in this little side room. A new nurse soon came in and took his blood pressure and temperature and informed us that the ER doctor would be there in a moment to check him out. At that time, one doctor did come in and took a look at him. A few minutes later he was moved over to the pediatric area of the ER. What impressed me was what happened after they moved him.

I was standing next to him when I turned my back for a moment. As I turned back around I noticed he started getting very lethargic. I immediately went out of the room and grabbed the first nurse that I saw, she was sitting at the nurse's station. I told her that my son was getting very lethargic.

She said, "No, he's just getting tired. It's very late at night."

I looked her in the eye and said to her, "You have to understand something. I've been sleeping next to this kid for twelve months. I know the difference between being tired, and being lethargic. He's not tired. He's lethargic." I didn't notice what she did but evidently she trusted my judgement and authority as a parent and hit some kind of button by the table she was standing behind. By the time I could physically turn around, there was an intern, three nurses and a couple of other people that I didn't even know in the room. I knew there was something wrong and was grateful the station nurse wasn't going to question it.

Literally, in a matter of seconds, there were ten people in the room starting IVs and putting him on oxygen. I don't think sixty seconds passed after I re-entered the room when the pediatric intensive care resident was there. There was also a respiratory therapist in the room. It was reassuring to watch them go to work so fast. Like I said, all this took place in a matter of sixty to a hundred and twenty seconds. The intensive care doctor never left Joshua's side after that. They immediately took him in and did a CAT Scan. They were trying to determine if he did have a stroke. It was at that time that, just to be on the safe side, they took him up to intensive care. That was our first experience with intensive care. Intensive care can be very intimidating. This one particular visit to intensive care was kind of nice, if there is a nice visit to intensive care. The beds in intensive care are in a bay kind of situation where everybody is side by side. They did have one little private room. They were slow that night, so they put Joshua in the private room. The biggest thing Joshua wanted to know about being in intensive care was how much money we were spending of the insurance company's funds. He got a kick out of every time we went to the emergency room or intensive care because he figured it was costing the insurance company big bucks and since we were making our premiums, he thought that was a cool thing. It's amazing what floats a kid's boat. That was one of his kid things. He figured the more they did to him, the more it cost the insurance company. The neurologist showed up. The oncologist showed up. Everybody who needed to be there was there to take care of him. What was determined later was that it was an adverse reaction to one of the chemo drugs. The end result was that he did not have a stroke, but that his physical problems were linked to an idiosyncratic neurologic toxicity of Ara-C. Sometimes the cure is worse than the disease.

The doctor told me that I could stay with Joshua in the ICU for a little longer, and that there was a waiting room down the hall. I said, "Yeah, whatever." Joshua didn't think that was going to be a great idea, which was obvious by his body language when they told me I could go wait in the waiting room. As it turns out, I wasn't having any of that either. I had brought a sleeping bag and I rolled it up underneath his bed and that's where I crawled up and went to sleep when he finally dozed off. In typical Joshua fashion, I was laying there on the concrete floor wondering if I really needed to do this, when I noticed out of the corner of my eye that he had positioned himself on the bed so he could look under it. Joshua, of course, did this, to make sure I was still there. At that point, I realized that the concrete wasn't so hard after all and it would do just fine. The following day everything worked itself out and he was transferred down to PEDHEMOC. He knew it was going to be a couple of weeks before he went home again. As before, anytime he went into PEDHEMOC, it was going to be ten days minimum before he was going to come home.

Going to the bathroom. People don't think a great deal about going to the bathroom. I never thought a great deal about going to the bathroom. Hospital stays could make going to the bathroom a real serious problem depending on the patient's condition. This is particularly true with multiple IV lines attached to the patient. Joshua didn't like just anybody helping him with private matters. He and I became in tune with each other's needs.

When he would be confined to bed either due to too many IV's or just because he was too weak or sick to get out of bed, he would have to use a bedpan or urinal. He would not allow the nurses to help him because he knew I would be showing up eventually and I would help him. The thing you need to understand, and I feel I did understand, having been a medic in the military, was that a patient has a right to dignity. I saw no reason not to afford the same dignity to my own son as I would to any patient. Touching my child's private parts (even though he was a teen-ager) was simply a medical necessity. Having to use the urinal sometimes required me to manipulate his penis to assist him. This was a simple patient procedure that didn't make me squeamish or cause any other reaction. The kid needed help, and when you have to go, you have to go. I felt bad for some of the other kids whose parents just couldn't bring themselves to get involved in the personal care of their child. I noticed other parents facing the same thing having a lot of problems. They either called the nurse or told the kid he had to fend for himself. It's not fair to say I didn't understand the feeling because I did understand it. What I didn't understand was how a parent could allow their feelings of insecurity or awkwardness to take over. The same thing would happen later if he needed to have a bowel movement, using a bedpan. If he needed someone to assist him, wiping himself, we just did it. He and I never had a discussion about whether or not he should be embarrassed. As his father, it was my job and I simply did it.

One time he became real concerned when the doctors and nurses wanted him to use a bedpan; he hated bedpans for bowel movements. God, he hated that with a passion. I could see that he was really apprehensive about using the bedpan. The doctors told him not to get out of bed. I was trying to figure out some way to help him when I saw that we had one of those chairs that you sit in when you take a shower. I took the bedpan and I taped it to the bottom of this shower chair. What really made it fun, for lack of a better word, was that he thought it was really great getting over on the doctors that he could sneak having a bowel movement just sliding off the bed right there and utilizing this chair. It took us about twenty minutes to rig this bedpan under the shower chair that we had gotten out of the bathroom. Little things like that, Joshua took great pride in and great enjoyment.

Often the bowel movements of patients on real heavy chemo are nothing more than water. The thing about it is if you keep wiping yourself, it tends to make your bottom really, really sore. So one of the things I showed him was that after you had a bowel movement, what you do is simply wipe yourself gently and then take a shower and utilize the water to wash yourself off. On several occasions, the bowel movements were so intense that he would get fecal matter on his legs when he couldn't control the process. During the really intense bowel movements fecal waste would get on his legs, socks, and other clothing that he might be wearing. I found it real important not to react to this. I would simply put on a pair of gloves and take a washcloth and clean him off. Take his socks, turn them inside out, and put them in the laundry bag that we always had there in the room. This cleaning process needed to be approached with a this-is-no-big-deal attitude. Usually what I would be doing while cleaning him up was talk about something else, a TV show or a movie, giving it no more importance than walking out in front of the house to get the mail.

Showering. This was another concern because as a teenager entering puberty, having to be bathed by your parents is not something a youngster is comfortable with. On several trips to the hospital, he would be extremely weak; to have to be assisted with showers was a concern to him. He absolutely did not want anybody involved in the showering process other than myself. He made that clear. He did not allow his mother, his sister, or any of the medical personnel to assist him with bathroom functions. I, on the other hand, was trying to figure out a way to preserve his dignity but get him clean. When he was really weak, I'd have him wear his underwear in the shower. I would then bathe him, wash his hair, under his arms and his legs and his stomach and body. Then after these areas were clean, I would close the curtain and tell him to now take off his shorts and wash his private areas. Then we would have to work out drying him off. I would take a towel and put it over my head, covering my eyes, because what you have to understand is that he's still connected to the IV pumps; there is still anywhere from two to three IV lines coming out of him. So I would stand there and control the IV lines. He would come out of the shower and he would wrap a towel around himself with my eyes being covered by this other towel. Then after he was covered up, I would remove the towel on my head and would dry him off. It actually worked quite well. It was functional and it preserved his dignity. So he never had to worry about me seeing his private parts. This whole methodology allowed him to preserve his dignity and allowed him to be comfortable in the process; we got him clean.

Patient care is all about assisting the patient whenever possible, and at the same time preserving their dignity. This became more evident one day when I noticed a parent dealing with her child at a local Kentucky Fried Chicken®. I was sitting there eating lunch when I noticed a couple with two children come in. The parents appeared to be in their early 30's and the children, two of them, a girl around eight and boy a little younger, sat about 10 feet from me. As I'm sitting there, the mother has the girl stand as the father approached with the food and demanded that she raise her shirt. For a second I couldn't figure out what they were doing. I soon realized that the little girl was diabetic and the mother was going to give her an insulin shot right there in front of God and everyone. This obviously was making the girl very upset. The parents' idea of how to control the situation was to berate the girl and to threaten her. I remember sitting there getting angry. I wanted to walk up to the mom and ask her if she wouldn't mind if someone sat her on the table here in front of everyone and did a pelvic exam on her. The parents had no idea that there might be a better way to handle this. I felt sad for the little girl. What would it have taken to get the food and walk out to the car? Or better yet, simply take care of her medical needs before entering the restaurant. Why do parents sometimes treat their kids worse than they themselves would like to be treated? I can truthfully say that we made sure that Joshua was never treated in such a nasty and hateful way.

Another matter that came up, which most readers will probably think is rather silly, is masturbation. Of course you will only think it is silly if you are never faced with the problem. If the following were your problem, you would then take it very seriously. Young teenage boys have physical needs, they're just entering puberty, and their sexual identification is coming into full hormonal swing. I noticed right off the bat that when Joshua was feeling really, really good in the hospital (as good as a leukemia patient can be), he became more active. For a leukemia patient, it wasn't that you had to be dying to be in the hospital. It was just that he had an infection or a fever and the doctors were concerned and had to give him antibiotics. Anytime Joshua was given antibiotics in IV fluids he was admitted to the hospital. So to look at him, he looked just fine and he felt fine, but he was nevertheless trapped in the hospital.

I could gauge how he was feeling late at night when he thought I was asleep, by the way he would stimulate himself. Now for those of you that think masturbation is not a healthy, normal function, you're wrong. It's a perfectly normal function. It's an absolutely normal function for a young teenage boy to masturbate. Some parents would react and say, "Oh, my God, we need to stop that before he goes blind." I would notice he would be doing this and I would take the basic military premise. You might ask what that would be! Well, you have what you would call a good roommate and a great roommate. A good roommate would sleep so soundly that if you were masturbating, he would not wake up. A great roommate would pretend that he was sleeping so soundly that he looked like he had not awakened. This became an indicator of how bad things were. When he was feeling good, he would be very aggressive. When things were not going well, he didn't do it at all. That was one of the little indicators I used to know how bad he was feeling. If you have a child that's going through this, you'll have to make your own decision. My own recommendation is that you make sure the child has privacy even to the point that you have to acknowledge to the child that you understand they're doing this and it's no big deal. Joshua and I had this discussion. Normally you would say you wouldn't even bring that up, but I took the position that he had to learn things rather quickly so we had a very frank discussion on the whole process. Different activities come at different times in a child's life. You usually have the luxury of telling a child "When you're older..." I wasn't taking anything for granted.

Another of life's lessons I felt I had to teach him was how to sneak into movie theaters. People call it movie hopping. Where you go into these multiplex cinemas where they have ten, twenty, thirty theaters all in the same theater, you buy one ticket, go in at noon and don't come out until midnight. This is one of the things that Joshua got the biggest kick out of doing. He would love to go in, buy one ticket, and see three or four movies. Since Joshua got sick, he needed to be in a very controlled environment, and basically the first year and a half of his treatment, he was hardly ever out of my sight. The first time we went to a movie together, we came out of the theater and he said this other movie starts in about twenty minutes, why don't we go over to see it. I said, "What do you want to do, just stand out here in the hallway?"

He said, "We'll just go in there and wait."

I said, "You can't do that because you could get caught."

So I said, "Well, let me show you how to do this." The way we would do it is we'd go into the first movie theater and take the newspaper with us. Then after we came out of the first showing, we would find out what else was still playing. We would go into an alternate theatre viewing a movie we had no interest in, waiting a couple of minutes until our second movie was starting down the hall. Once the second movie started, we'd move to that theater and watch our second feature. To be quite honest, this really, really irritated my wife. She saw it as stealing. I didn't see it that way. I guess my logic was it wasn't hurting the movie theater that much. The biggest thing about it is that Joshua got a kick out of it. Joshua thought this was the neatest thing since peanut butter and as long as he enjoyed it and it gave him pleasure, by God, we were going to do it.

When he wasn't in the hospital, this is what we would do on Sunday. Thursdays were also a great movie day. Thursdays because there was never anything on TV and Sunday because it just seemed appropriate. Sunday afternoon, sneak into the movie theaters and stay as long as we could "sneak." I think the best we did was see like four movies in a day. By the time we got done, we could hardly see. We did this once in a movie theater in Freehold and when we came out of the second movie that we had seen, for some reason, there were police officers in the lobby. I'm sure they weren't there for us but it was kind of fun to pretend that they were. We sneaked down the back hall, out the back of the theater, around the building, and to the car. After entering the car, we took off real quick. That gave him a big adrenaline rush. You find that those simple little things in life tend to make all the other misery bearable.

# CHAPTER VI

# Pepsee

They say nothing happens by accident. Everything has a purpose. We had a couple of Rottweilers. The female's name was Pepsee, and her brother's name was Smooch. A couple of years earlier we had to have Smooch put down because of hip dysplasia. About nine or ten months into Joshua's treatment, Pepsee suffered the same type of condition as her brother. She could hardly walk anymore. Without being cruel, having to put the dog to sleep is the best thing that ever happened. Before you think I'm cold-hearted and insane, what you have to understand is that Joshua took Pepsee's death very hard. What happened is that we had to tell him that Pepsee had to be put down. This really bothered Joshua a great deal. My wife actually told Joshua what had to be done with Pepsee because I chickened out. I couldn't tell him. A problem developed that he had to take his medication that day and he refused to take it. Knowing that Pepsee was to be taken to the Vet was very upsetting to him. My wife called me at work, had me come home, and told me that he wouldn't take his medication. We did allow him time to say goodbye to the dog but then he got very depressed. Joshua and I started to get into an argument about him taking his medication. Joshua told me he didn't want to take it. I told him that he had to. This exchange of words went back and forth. I was trying to walk that fine line between being a consoling parent and being a parent that in fact knew he had to take these drugs.

Joshua was sitting in my chair in front of the TV and I was standing off to the corner in what would be the dining room area trying to convince him, knowing all the time that he was upset, that he had to take this medication. He just steadfastly refused to do it. I finally came upon an idea. I looked at him and said, "I know you're upset, but have you ever stopped to think that maybe this is upsetting for me too? Did you ever stop to think that I needed to be comforted and I needed a hug?" Well, it was like a light went on in his head as he realized that **he** needed to take care of **me**. He came over and just wrapped his arms around me. It didn't take him more than a second to realize I was crying. I loved the dog too and there was nothing we could do about putting her to sleep. He cradled me in his arms, and then a moment later stated that he was going to go back to his room. I saw no need to push the medication thing just then. It wouldn't matter if he took it then or maybe a little bit later.

I asked, "Do you want me to go back to the room with you?" His response was something to the effect of, do what you think you need to do. So I followed him back to his room and watched as he lay down on his bed. At this point, he was starting to sniffle a little bit and tears were coming out of his eyes. I remember crawling up in the bed next to him and just wrapping my arms around him. Joshua was about a hundred and forty pounds, I guess. I'm about two hundred and fifty pounds. I just engulfed him in my arms and held him there as he cried.

He started to understand how important he was when he noticed I was ignoring my cell phone and pager. Before when they would go off, everyone would have to be quiet and not interrupt. Everyone in the family knew that business came first. As I lay there holding him, my pager and cell phone went off and I ignored them. Repeatedly this happened during that afternoon. Finally after what seems like a dozen pages and an equal number of cell phone calls, I went to get the home phone and brought it back to the bedroom. I don't know why I brought it back to the bedroom; it just seemed that's the way it developed. I called the office and told my secretary to leave me alone until I called her. I crawled back on top of the bed with Joshua, wrapped my arms around him again, and felt him melt into my embrace. I knew that at that point he understood how important he was. He understood that I was forsaking all the business and any potential moneymaking things that were happening that day because it was more important that I stayed with him. About an hour or two later, Pat came home. Pat had taken the dog to the vet and for Pepsee, the job was done. When she walked to the back of the house, and saw us in his room, the look on her face was one of surprise. Pat stayed in the doorway without saying anything for a few moments, then left and returned to the living room area. The process of lying with and holding my son while he cried, he never did stop crying, lasted approximately six and a half to seven hours. I say Pepsee dying was the best thing that ever happened because after she died, and after that day of just holding him for hours, Joshua was never afraid to hold or be held. When he felt bad he would simply pull himself up to the chair that I was sitting in and would literally pick up my arm and put it around him. He would hug his mother. He would get this silly voice almost like an Elmer Fudd® type accent and just say, "I love you." He became much happier, much calmer, and much more physically affectionate after that day.

So I have no doubt that somewhere up in heaven Pepsee is looking down on us and in her own doggy way, understands that her greatest achievement was dying for a 14-year-old boy.

One of the interesting by-products of Joshua being confined for the first twelve months of his illness, and not being able to leave the house, due to a suppressed immune system, was the learning of patience. Joshua got a kick out of people when he went back to school who were very upset when they got grounded for a week or a weekend or they couldn't watch a certain TV show. He spent twelve months essentially being grounded, being locked up in the house. He wasn't allowed to go anywhere. He didn't go to the malls. If he did go somewhere, which was rare, it had to be with me. After a year or so, the only place he could go was to the movies late at night. We would go into the late showing of a movie that had been out for several weeks because we knew there wouldn't be a crowd. One of the things you want to do is what they call a **ten-foot circle**. Don't let anybody within ten feet of the child. This barrier was easier to maintain during the late night movies. He seemed to enjoy that quite a bit. The other thing he really got into was the Sega® type games. *Mortal Combat II*® was his favorite. Being an expert at *Mortal Combat II* became a small problem.

This problem with *Mortal Combat II* manifested itself later when he finally was able to go out. As we were able to visit the local malls, Joshua would always want to head to the arcade. I'd give him a couple of dollars, and into the bowels of the arcade he would go. It was a real pain in the butt waiting for him, but he enjoyed it and the reason for the outing was for him to have some fun. The only problem was, he started hustling kids with *Mortal Combat II*. It was quite amazing to watch him. He would sit there and play a very casual game. Sooner or later some poor kid, the mark: person being hustled, would walk up and ask if he could play and Joshua would let him. Joshua would hold back and let the other player accumulate points. Joshua refrained from killing his opponent's character, choosing only to offer up a minor string of assaults against his opponent's computer generated hero. After the mark thought that he could beat him, the foolish kid would offer to bet a quarter, fifty cents, seventy-five cents, sometimes even a dollar. Joshua would wait to do his stuff till it got up to a dollar a game. Once the bet was made and before the mark could blink his eyes, the character would be dead. The thing Joshua got a chuckle out of was that if anybody gave him a hard time, he would just say talk to his partner and his opponent would turn around and I'd be standing there. I remember one time Joshua did this in the East Brunswick Mall; he started hustling some kids. I suggested that he'd better be more careful about hustling the inner city kids. He let some guy beat him on a couple of games and the other kid boasted he would bet Joshua a couple of dollars and he would take all his money. Joshua believed the other kid to be arrogant. Joshua said fine, but instead of slowly beating him, Joshua gave this kid about thirty seconds and killed off three of his characters. This fast action really pissed the guy off. I thought there was going to be a little confrontation when Joshua stated, "You could get in my face with the problem, but you've got to get in his face too." Of course his disgruntled opponent turned around and I was standing there. This wasn't the greatest pastime for him to be involved in. I figured while he was going through this treatment I would allow him to have his little bit of happiness. This hustling never got outrageous. The most I think anybody ever lost was a couple of dollars to him. But it was just a wonder to watch him hustle these kids with the *Mortal Combat II* series.

One thing I haven't talked too much about is how much the child should be told about his particular disease. Joshua was thirteen when he was diagnosed. A thirteen-year-old can understand anything if you take the time to explain it right. We chose the path of telling him everything and keeping no secrets from him. Obviously if the child is four or five years old, this is not going to be an appropriate response. My wife and I had decided we would keep nothing from him, and that was a really good thing because all through his treatment, Joshua knew he could trust his doctors. Joshua could tell if his doctors were holding something back from him. If they did, he would discuss his concerns with his mom and me. Everyone soon came to understand, including Joshua, that his mother and I would be up front and honest with him. The doctors realized that they should answer his questions very frankly. In fact, one of the discussions we had with the doctors at the very onset of treatment was how much of his condition and treatment did we want the medical staff to discuss with Joshua. My opinion was that it was his life and anything that involved his life should be discussed with him. During his entire treatment, we kept no secrets from him. He knew at every given point when things were going good, when things were going bad. That's just the way we chose to handle it. I would never take the position that a parent was handling it wrong if they withheld information from a child. One thing I have learned over the last few years is that how people handle their own family is strictly up to them. There is no right or wrong way; it's just the way you choose, remembering always to follow your gut instinct, and not be swayed by others' doubts.

Television became very important to Joshua. Not only was it an escape from boredom, but it became a forum for him and me to begin discussions. TV became a great tool to begin communication between him and me. As stated before, Joshua never liked to talk until after midnight. Our routine was that we had certain shows that we always watched together. What was amazing about it, even though I might not be home, he would tape these shows so that we could watch them together. Every time he would do that it would remind me of an old, old episode of *Eight Is Enough*. I think it was a reunion show. The father character was feeling depressed and the daughter, who was now grown up and had children of her own, went to the refrigerator and made him a sandwich of peanut butter and sardines and then served it to him at the kitchen table. This was taking place late at night. He looked at her and said, "I really hate peanut butter and sardine sandwiches."

Her response was, "But that's what I used to make you when I was a little kid."

He responded back, "Well, if your son made you a peanut butter and sardine sandwich, what would you do?" Of course the obvious answer was that she would eat it. Joshua would tape television shows that were entertaining but had he not taped it, I never would have watched it. He did have some favorites. He loved *Ally McBeal*. He always made sure that the *Star Trek*® episodes were taped for me. *Deep Space 9*® was on at the time. So was *Star Trek Voyager*®. So whenever he had a chance, he would tape those for me and we would sit down later and watch them together. By and large, another favorite TV show was *Law and Order*. *Law and Order* re-runs would go on at eleven-thirty. For some reason, he just latched onto that show and it didn't matter if it was repeat after repeat after repeat. He would sit there knowing that "I" wanted to watch *Law and Order*. There were many nights, particularly when he wasn't feeling good, that we would stay up together until he fell asleep in front of the TV.

## Sleeping Arrangements

Sleeping arrangements were another thing that was rather unique. When Joshua first came home after being in the hospital a couple of months, there was a concern to keep an eye on him because he was still new to the treatment and we didn't know what to expect. Joshua's mom and I knew that he had to be watched rather closely. Plus when he came home, he usually had IV fluid that had to be administered to him via IV pumps, which required a great deal of maintenance. The pumps were constantly getting air bubbles in the lines. When the bubbles formed, the alarm would go off, the pump stop, and we'd have to purge the line and check everything. We got pretty good at that. The other thing that required maintenance was a surgically implanted IV line in his chest. This line is used for both IV fluids and various drugs. These lines have to be flushed every day and maintained because they are just like any other kind of wound; proper wound care was a must. You constantly have to maintain a vigilance to keep infection away. That's the secret about kids with leukemia. It's not the leukemia you have to worry about all the time; it's infection because the immune system is supressed. In our living room we have a hide-a-way sofa. This is the L-shaped type with kick-up chairs. Joshua finally did come home. He slept on the fold-out bed part of the couch. The balance of the couch is where I slept. It was over a year into his treatment before we actually felt comfortable putting him back in his own room. His room was at the end of the hall just across from mine. Still most nights we would stay up late watching TV and he would talk about everything and then he would fall asleep on the couch. After he would fall asleep, I would go back to my room. Some nights he would go back to his room, others he would stay right where he was. He was never quite comfortable going to sleep on his own for at least twelve months into his treatment. Mostly he fell asleep while watching TV. I would just stay up until he did fall asleep, then I would throw a blanket on him and depart to my room. I guess that was the equivalent of reading someone to sleep at night when they're a little child. The only difference being that in the morning I'd have to go to work and he would sleep in till twelve or one o'clock. Joshua never was an early riser.

One of the hardest things about taking our two kids anywhere together was Kristin would want to get up and go at the crack of dawn and Joshua and I liked to sleep in. Kristin wanted to run, run, run. Joshua's idea of a fabulous vacation would be to watch TV, stay up a little late at night and sleep in the morning and don't bother him. These two philosophies were not compatible.

One of the things you have to be aware of is that the medication that kids are on will do a lot of different things. Chemo could make him sick as a dog. Some side effects can weigh heavy on your ability to cope. Probably the hardest thing to deal with is the combination of hormones in their own body and the steroids that they start taking. **Mood swings** is probably not an appropriate label for the condition, but the problem is because of the combination of the hormones and the steroids. Sometimes Joshua would get extremely cranky and argumentative. If you think the Incredible Hulk® had a personality problem, you should try a teenager on steroids with hormones racing through his body! Even though he knew this was a drug side effect, it really didn't help much as far as trying to keep him mellow. I have no pat answer in telling you how to deal with this particular medication side effect. The biggest thing you've got to remember is that no matter how many times your child starts bouncing off the wall, you've got to understand that these medication side effects have nothing to do with your child. They may say things that are hurtful and mean. The stress of the situation is going to show its ugly head in the form of actions that are out of character and by anyone's definition inappropriate behavior. Deal with the situation, as best you can, and remember this too shall pass. Of course taking Joshua out and letting him have an expensive cigar always seemed to aid the passing of these bouts of **hyperactivity/nastiness**.

# CHAPTER VII

# Telling People
# My Child Has Leukemia

We know, Joshua knows, now it's time to tell others. If you think it was hard sitting in the room while the doctor informed us that our child had leukemia, you are right. However, the next thing that's almost equally hard is that you have to tell loved ones. I'm not talking about the people you work with, the newspaper boy, the lady at the local shop. Uncles, aunts, sister, grandparents, friends of your child, and all those other people who have grown up with him need to be told.

The first person you have to tell is the child. This is not going to be one of those let me kiss it and all will be better talks. I remember telling him that the next few years would require a lot of time at the hospital and that he had leukemia, which was a form of cancer. His first reaction was to say, "fine," but he did not want to talk about it, and he didn't. I asked him if he had any questions and he responded with no. I asked him if he understood what I said and he stated, "yes." At the time he simply would not, or could not discuss it. I soon learned that Joshua liked to do all his talking late at night when everything was calm (midnight to 2 a.m.).

Joshua liked to be macho. But, when it came to sleeping in the hospital at night, he never once stated that he should be allowed to stay by himself. That's the way it was; when Joshua was in the hospital I was in the hospital; that was my job. One thing that helped was keeping a small over-night bag packed. The bag should contain toilet items and a change of clothes. A cellular phone is also a must. Having a cellular phone will make communicating with family much easier. Remember not to use the phone or any other electrical equipment, around the heart monitors. It interferes with the equipment's operation. Another thing that you will want to have is several of the calling cards for the in-room phone. Make sure that the cards do not expire even if you do not use them. At Robert Wood they gave them to the kids for free; nice perk.

The night we found out Joshua had leukemia my wife told his sister Kristin; I was at the hospital. As I understand it, she did not take the information very well and spent most of the night crying. A few days later, when Kristin noticed my wife was packing many things for Joshua to have at the hospital, she offered a joking remark. Kristin asked why her mother had not done all these extra things when she was in the hospital. Pat responded, "When you were in the hospital, you were not dying." My wife always felt bad for saying that. I know Kristin meant it as a joke, but it is one of those memories that linger on.

We found out on a Friday that Joshua definitely had leukemia. We had decided to wait on telling people until we knew for sure what he had. We now knew. I needed to tell my parents. Since David, my brother, and my parents were in Atlantic City having a much-deserved rest, I didn't see the need to call them and ruin their weekend as well. I figured over the next couple of years we would get enough memories of things as they happened. I didn't need to create one pairing Atlantic City and Joshua's illness.

The first person I tried to call was my youngest brother, Jimmy. It seemed every time I called, he was not home and his wife Lorna would answer the phone. Ever time Lorna would answer the phone, I would just tell her that I was looking for Jimmy. I did not want to tell her about Joshua until they were both together. I knew Jimmy would be upset, but what I did not count on was how upset Lorna would be. I later learned that one of her friends had a child with leukemia. It seemed I underestimated her feelings. It turns out that she cried as much as the rest of us. I never did tell Jimmy myself. Jimmy found out, as did David and Ricky my oldest brother, from my mother.

Telling parents. My wife offered to tell my parents. It was nice of her to offer me a way out. I felt it was my responsibility to tell my parents. After they returned from Atlantic City, I called them. Every time I called, my father was home by himself or my mother was home by herself, so to tell them alone would not be smart. So I called, and called, and called. Finally about the middle of the afternoon on Monday, I called and got my mother. She told me my father had just returned home from his outing. I had called from the car as I was leaving the hospital. The hospital is about two miles away, so I told her I would be over in a few minutes. On the phone, I purposely did not tell them there was a problem. It seems my mother has great insight; she knew something was wrong. I went over in my head how I would tell them. I rehearsed every sentence down to the last comma. I knew it would be important that I keep a level head and a straight face when telling them. I went over and over what I would say, even as I pulled up to their house. I should have known my mother would suspect something. When I pulled into the driveway, she was already standing at the doorway with the door open. I got out of the car and started to walk towards the door. It seemed all my intentions to stay calm were a waste. With every step I took towards my Mother,

I started to cry more and more. I could feel my face crunching and my eyes weeping. The closer I got to the door, the more I could not control the tears. I could see my mother's face. She looked down from the porch and asked what was wrong.

All I could say was, "Joshua has leukemia." Her immediate response was, "Oh, no." Then she started to cry. While this was happening my father was sitting in his special chair just next to the door. He got up from his chair and walked a few steps towards us. I remember looking him in the eye and saying Joshua has cancer. I always see my father as a strong man even though he is in his '70s. But at that moment he looked like a little waste of a man. He just stood stunned, in shock, stooped his shoulders and cried.

In all my years, I have seen my father cry three times. The first time caught me by surprise. I had first entered the Army in 1972. I had not been gone too long when I came home unannounced from Basic Training and surprised them. When I came into the house, he gave me a hug and just started to cry. At the time I never understood it or appreciated the depth of his feelings. It takes being a father to understand. The second time I saw him cry was the same day. He had purchased a scratch-off ticket for the lottery. As we sat in the car, he scratched off the covering and he found he had won two dollars. He started to cry again, saying he was the luckiest man in the world, he had his son home and won two dollars. I am now 45 years old and a father of two, and I understand. The news about Joshua had become the third time I saw him cry.

We sat in the living room and I told them as much as I knew. I could tell my mother was handling the information reasonably well, but my father did not. He would start and stop crying the whole time. Finally he just lowered his head and asked God that he'd be taken and not Joshua. Then he professed, "Joshua had his whole life ahead of him and that I'm old." At the time the only thing I could do was get up and hold him, and tell him no one was going anywhere.

That 10 minutes I was there seemed like an hour. My wife had offered to tell my parents. In hindsight part of me wished I had let her. I tried several more times to find my brothers to tell them but they were never around. Finally I asked my parents to explain the situation to them. Having my mother and father tell my brothers was definitely wimping out. What can I say? I just could not beat up on myself again anymore this day.

Jimmy found out when he came to my parents' house to pick up some equipment. My father told him that my mother needed to talk to him about something. He suspected it had to do with moving some of his landscaping supplies. When he went into the house, my mother told him Joshua was in the hospital with leukemia. At first he stared at her in disbelief. It took Jimmy about 20 minutes to get up to the hospital where I was with my son. Jimmy and I met in the hall. His first reaction was definitely anger. I could see he was trying not to cry but he was not very successful. I placed my arms around him and held him briefly but he just could not simply stand there, so he started to walk short steps back and forth under the sign that said Pediatric Hematology & Oncology. After he calmed down a bit, he went to see Joshua. He did a very good job of maintaining his composure. It was later that night that I saw David. When I first saw him, we were inside the double swinging doors where you enter the clinic. I motioned for him to go outside the clinic with me. We went into the hallway and he asked me how I was doing. "Not well," I responded. I could see he wanted to cry but he surmised that I needed to more. So he wrapped his arms around me and I let go like a small child who had fallen off a bike.

After a few minutes we both went back into the clinic and stayed with Joshua. As I remember it, 24 hours later is when Ricky, my older brother, who lives in California, found out. My mother told him when he called the house. The next day Joshua had this really large basket of stuff delivered to him from my older brother. You could always count on Rick for things like that.

The next person that had to be told was Erin. Erin was the mom of Joshua's best friend Ernie, not to mention she was also like a second mom to Joshua. My wife told her. As I understand it, she became very upset. When she would come up to the hospital and visit you could tell she had been crying. It was very hard for her not to cry when she was there. In fact every time she came to see Joshua, she would cry. Erin told her son little Ernie about Joshua's condition. Little Ernie was a very important factor in Joshua's treatment.

As soon as Pat had Joshua's diagnosis confirmed, she called her mother in Colorado. I was glad she was the one telling the rest of the people we knew. Telling people, to me, is like walking over hot coals, and I was glad to let my wife do it.

Everyone else that had to be told the news would have to wait. There were other family members, cousins and such. For the most part, those folks were not in a position to have day-to-day contact with Joshua. The inner circle had been informed and the rest would be gotten at a later time.

As you will see later in this writing, many people were not told that my son was sick. Joshua wanted his illness kept private. Joshua's instructions in many areas differed from the way I might do things, but it was his life and we did as he asked.

# CHAPTER VIII

# Meeting People
# Along the Way to Recovery

While Joshua was going through treatment, there were a lot of people that we met that were just totally remarkable. This section of the book is going to deal with all those people. Many of the folks I will be writing about will be family members. Others will just be plain folks, much like the person that you sat next to on your last plane ride or at the movies. Still others will be some of the many folks that I worked with and came into contact with as I traveled with Joshua. Each person we came into contact with offered his or her own unique thing when it came to Joshua and me. In this writing I tried to remember all the good in people, and with as much deliberateness I tried to forget the bad.

Obviously the people that had the most impact would be his mother and sister. Kristin is almost four years older than Joshua, and as of this writing, she now has a family of her own, a wonderful son named Dakota, Koty for short, and a new, just as wonderful little girl named Iliana. Kristin started her family early. One of the things that Joshua would say to his mom was that if things didn't work out, she would still have Dakota. Every time he would say that, it would really sadden Pat. I believe he made these statements to make her feel better, but just as equally, I believe that he said it so no matter what the outcome; he wanted people to know that life would go on.

If I've learned one thing, I've learned that each person brings their own strengths to the situation, and no one can dictate how people will or will not face a dilemma such as treating a child for cancer. Pat is a pretty strong lady. She truly is very much more a pillar of strength than I am. I found it at times to be very difficult to deal with the fact that I had a son that was sick. Pat, on the other hand, went day by day, or as we say one day at a time. Pat was delegated to make sure he took his pills and other medical treatments. It was obvious that she got the worst of the health care duties. She also got to play the heavy; many times she was the bad guy and I would get to come along and save the day. She would tell our son that he couldn't go somewhere or do some activity and Joshua would resign himself to that. Then I would come home and he would want to go somewhere and I would take him with me. Pat had the bad guy role in all of this. Bad guy role. Who in their right mind would want that role? To be honest, I can't tell you if we ever discussed it. It just seemed that's the way it worked out.

When treating Joshua, everyone just seemed to take on different aspects of the care. As I stated before, we never really discussed roles, even though I'm probably arrogant enough to say that I think I forced Pat into hers. I took the role that I thought was important to me, the one that I thought I could handle the best. Pat never said much about it and just seemed to go along with the flow. Over the years of our marriage, she has gone along with me on many things. I guess that is why I love her so much. Every time we moved, I would change careers. When we had to uproot when I was in the military, she went along without complaining. She is responsible for creating a good family. For all her strengths, I have to commend her. She didn't get to have a lot of fun with Joshua during his treatment. One thing he truly enjoyed was whenever his white counts were okay and his blood work showed that he could be around people, he would ask to be taken to the mall. Pat would stop whatever she was doing and take him. She would then change her schedule around however she had to so that she could pick him up at the appointed time. It didn't matter what she had planned; she would simply interrupt her day, drop all things and take him. That's just the way she is.

When it came time for him to go back to school, she didn't want him to be bothered with the bus. So when he was able to attend school, she would drive him every day. She didn't want him dealing with the one-hour bus commute. All the things that everyday parents did, she did, but then she went above and beyond. It is hard to deny your child the simple things like going places and enjoying outings that most kids take for granted.

When Joshua's blood work was okay, Pat allowed him to walk over to the mall after school. With work and everything, it was a crazy inconvenience to her to later pick him up. By this time we felt he was old enough to go to the mall by himself, as long as he was with a select group of friends. These were the kids we entrusted with Joshua's safety. These "mall friends" that he traveled with were the select few who knew of his situation, knew to protect him, and to keep me informed should anything go wrong. We relied on these friends to take care of him. Joshua's friends could always be counted on. Joshua became quite a mall rat. In his travels to the mall, he got to know many people. Some, like him, hung out at the mall, and still others were there as a source of employment.

This extended family became very important to him. There's no getting around that. With regard to the mall trips themselves, I think Pat felt that this was the one thing she could do for our son that nobody else could. I know he appreciated it.

There are many things that she did for others as well. If anyone needed something, Pat was the one to call. As far as myself, whenever I needed a break, she would help me take it, saying, "Just go." At one point in his treatment, things got somewhat hectic and I just needed a couple of days.

Pat said, "Go." I can't imagine too many wives telling a husband, "Just go."

I worked for several years for Carnival Cruise Lines® as a stage hypnotist, so I knew most of the boats. I would grab a boat for three days and of course Pat held everything together while I was gone. Pat also took our son to all his clinic appointments. This required her to sit there for hours. That's one thing about treating a cancer child. A lot of appointments, a lot of heartache, a lot of hurry up and wait. A lot of sitting, watching your child in pain and suffering, and not feeling good. I'm glad my wife was around to do all that. Quite honestly, she handles those things better than I do. I have a hard time taking the dogs to the vet when they need treatment.

One of the first little hiccups we had was when one of the videos came back late one day and the girl at the local video shop gave Pat a hard time. She came home to me and was a little upset about the hard time she was given. With Joshua in the hospital, she didn't need the extra grief. I went down and I met a gentleman named Toby. He worked there. I walked in the store and said I needed to talk to him. He took me in the back and I explained to him that Joshua had leukemia and was in the hospital. That the employees needed to understand that we would be renting videos and that sometimes they would come back late just because of the logistics of the situation. We would expect to be charged late fees. I really didn't care; my wife was not to be hassled about why the tapes weren't back on time. Toby turned out to be a good friend. After that meeting with Toby, we were never hassled concerning the late returns. Toby helped us out whenever he could. As far as the late charges, sometimes they'd charge us, sometimes they didn't. Their efforts were always appreciated. Whenever we did get late charges, we didn't feel slighted in the least. They really treated us good. Pat particularly appreciated not being hassled anymore about the late returns. It seemed like Pat always took the position that she was in the background of life's goings on. Like I said, I don't think we ever discussed it. It kind of got delegated to her. She took over and stood in the shadows. I got to go places, do things, and have fun with Joshua while she kept all the day to day activities running smooth. Well, as smooth as they can when dealing with a child with cancer.

When Joshua was going for surgery, we would both be there but I would always go with him into the operating room, stay with him until the medication kicked in, then I'd come out and we'd go to the waiting area. The waiting area was like a big fish bowl. I'll never understand why they do it that way. There are numerous chairs and a TV there, with some reading material and a "hostess" of sorts that keeps track of who is there. The walls are big panes of glass. People walk by knowing it is the surgical waiting area and it is obvious that they all wonder about the people in the "fish tank." It is quite disquieting just sitting on show for the entire world to see. If I were ever going to make a suggestion to the hospital, it would be that they'd change the surgical waiting room into a more private area, maybe add Internet access. Add a couple of TVs because someone always has the financial news on. At least half the people in the waiting room don't seem to be the type interested in financial news. Family members and loved ones are nervous, scared, and they're uptight, but I think they would appreciate having a TV on in the background. The hospital should definitely isolate them from the rest of the hospital. Sitting there being watched is a very uncomfortable feeling. I took all these things in stride. During the entire time Joshua was treated, I don't think Pat had a single day to herself. Between the clinic visits and all the other things necessary to keep the household going, she didn't go anywhere or do anything for herself. All she did was take care of Kristin, Koty, Joshua, and me. She made sure she was around so if we needed something, she would be available.

Pat got a notice for Jury Duty. She's always wanted to do Jury Duty but that wasn't going to happen. We ended up getting a note from the doctor to get excused because she had to care for Joshua. Just recently she got a notice for Jury Duty and I casually suggested that we run our business and she needs to be around. Pat put the kibosh on that real quick. She really wanted to do it the first time, but Joshua was in treatment so she couldn't. Come hell or high water, she was going to serve this time. That's the kind of person she is. She has a very strong sense of responsibility whether it's family matters or just things she believes in.

Kristin became very important to her brother ever since day one when he was told he was sick. She became his confidante and above all became a source of food delivery whenever he was in the hospital. Kristin spent a great deal of time with him during all his hospital stays. She also was the one delegated to stay with him whenever I couldn't be there at night. Delegated. What a silly word to use. Kristin insisted that she be the one to stay with Joshua when I couldn't be there. Any discussion otherwise would have been a joke and a waste of good air.

Other people involved during this process had a great impact not only on Joshua but also me, my family, and the people around them. There is no hierarchy intended here but just a methodology of trying to remember everybody involved. So the next person I'm going to be talking about is actually my father. My father is a pretty strong individual. He went to visit Joshua quite a bit. Joshua enjoyed his visits. He'd always get a gleam in his eyes when grandpa was coming up. One of the great things about grandpa coming up to his room was food. Even when Joshua was sick as a dog, he could eat. After one of many medical procedures, and after Joshua had been moved back to his room, Peggy the play specialist stopped in to check on him. Looking at Joshua, still under the influence of the anesthesia, Peggy made the comment that when Joshua woke up from the procedure that the last thing on his mind would be food. I told her she was wrong. Peggy's response was that she would bet us a dollar she was right. As soon as the meds wore off, the first thing Joshua asked for was a cheese steak. The dollar was taped to his wall for a long time. Joshua was predictable.

Grandpa was always bringing stuffed shells. Joshua really liked those, too. If nothing else, he knew he was going to eat well if my father showed up at the hospital. My father never liked to talk about how serious all this stuff could be, so we didn't.

My mother is an interesting person, full of love and charity. She didn't go to the hospital much. I think it just hurt too much to be up there. She never shied away from Joshua. When Joshua was at grandma's house, it was all hugs, love, kisses, and food. She made all kinds of food for him, which is really good because he could really eat. Like I said before, he really liked the biscuits. Nobody had any opinions because she didn't go up to the hospital often. It's just the way she handles things.

Ricky is my older brother. There were a lot of years when Ricky and I were growing up that we actually didn't get along very well. As we got older and had families, I think we started to get along better. We certainly have more things in common now. Ricky was hard to grow up behind, only because of the limitations I put on myself. Ricky was the proverbial rocket scientist. Actually, he is a rocket scientist. His current job requires that he coordinate the efforts of those who make the satellites and those who make the rockets or launch vehicles, as they are called. Ricky has the gift of being extremely intelligent. I have him to thank for my graduate work because one of the reasons I pursued my second Master's Degree was partially so I could say I had more education than he did. Even though now, it seems pretty childish. Ricky has given me a number of things over the years but the two things that stand out in my mind more than any other are first, a Swiss Army knife he gave me just before I went into Ranger School. That was the first memorable thing he ever gave me. Of course there were other things he gave me for various holidays. But the Swiss Army knife he gave me was something that he set out to buy based on the things going on in my life. I still have it. I carried that knife through Ranger School and Special Forces training. When I went to Ranger School most of the guys carried these double edged dagger-type knives which were limited in their use for what we needed. I carried a deer axe, which is a small two-pound axe my father gave me when I joined Scouts, and the

Swiss Army knife that my brother had given me. Perfect combination for what I needed. One of the red plastic sides fell off and I was told I could send it back to the company and they would repair it or replace it. I've never done that because I was always afraid they would replace it. I want this knife. I didn't want a new one. That was one of the things that he gave me that I will always treasure. Once while in "Phase One" of Special Forces training (there are three phases) I thought I had lost the knife. I told everyone I needed help in finding it and they all laughed. I told them my brother had given it to me prior to entering Ranger School. On hearing that, everyone then stepped in to help find it; we did. They all understood a brother's love.

The second thing Ricky gave me was the care and loving he gave my son while all this hospital stuff was going on. He was always keeping track of Joshua's progress. He would send him books and puzzles. Ricky impressed me.

The next person on the list is David. David is the number three son. I'm number two. David was the "go to" person if I needed to talk to someone over a beer. David was always good at getting Joshua to laugh when he had to stay in the hospital.

Jimmy is brother number four. Of all the brothers, Jimmy and I have the most in common. I don't mean this as a put-down to anyone else. We run our own businesses and we bitch, moan, and complain about our various clients. Jimmy is quite remarkable. Jimmy takes everything to heart and he gets upset over everything, which is probably to his credit. He's somewhat emotional. He worries a lot. Jimmy had more contact with Joshua than anybody in my family simply because he and I would many times go to the movies together and Joshua would go with us. If I was with Joshua and we'd go out to dinner, I'd ask Joshua, "You want to call Uncle Jimmy?" He'd follow with, "It's up to you. If you want to call him, call him." Sometimes I would, sometimes I wouldn't. When Jimmy and I had plans to go out, Jimmy always understood that if Joshua wanted to go somewhere, Joshua took precedence. A lot of times when Jimmy and I would go to the movies, Joshua would end up coming with us, or vice versa. Joshua and I would head out to the movies and Jimmy would be grabbed up. We would start to the movies and I would say to Joshua, "This is a movie that Uncle Jimmy would like." He would say, "If you want to call him, call him." The call usually led to Joshua and I going to pick up Uncle Jimmy. Jimmy didn't like to drive at the end of the day. Jimmy was constantly checking up on Joshua to see if everything was all right. He would see him when he could. It was a little awkward for Jimmy, though, only because he worked in landscaping a lot and he could never visit the hospital going directly from work. Jimmy would have to go over to my mother's house, shower up, change his clothes, and then he would go to the hospital. He did that quite often. Joshua appreciated it. Joshua, I know, appreciated going along with Jimmy and me to the movies, dinner, and things like that. Being treated as an equal is an aspect of our travels that I cannot stress enough. As often as the situation would allow Joshua was treated as an adult. Joshua was not tagging along with the group, he was part of the group.

There were a lot of other people that had a strong effect on Joshua. The nurses that cared for him were really great. It takes a very special person to work with children that are facing serious illness and possible death. It would be unfair to say he had a favorite. But the truth of it is, at one point he liked all of them. At one point, he hated all of them. Joshua's attitude toward the medical staff was predicated on what they were doing to him at that particular time. It's just like his doctors. Some days his relationship with a particular doctor was great, other days he felt put upon by them. The one doctor he definitely liked the best was Dr. Michaels. I think he liked her the best because she would talk to him, and not down to him. It's not to say the other doctors wouldn't talk to him, but somehow Joshua and Dr. Michaels clicked the best. Whenever he was admitted to the hospital he took great delight in giving the staff a hard time. I would tell him to let up and his only response was, "Yea, right."

Pearl is a woman that owns the computer store. Pearl is quite remarkable. She was extremely emotional when she found out about Joshua. The strange thing about it was that she really knew very little about him other than the fact that he is my son. Whenever we called, she would always ask about him. She would always assure me that Joshua was in her prayers. There are some people that say, "Well, I'll put you in my prayers" and it's said with no more weight than "How are you? Where are you going today? Did you go to the mall?" Pearl truly cared, and I have no doubt that Joshua was mentioned prominently and often in her prayers. Her husband Pat is also quite a guy. Pat and I did business over the years with nothing more than a handshake.

Some people we would never see again. Still, they were so important to us. I'll never forget the times during Joshua's treatment, I needed a break. I'm sure my wife needed a break too, but she always took it as her responsibility to keep the home fire burning and stand by in case anything happened. Every time I would need a day off or something, she would say, "Nothing is going to happen. Go. Worst case scenario, we'll call you and you'll find a way back home." One interesting thing about traveling that I had not anticipated: fear. I never was afraid of dying before. Now the thought of dying and leaving Joshua alone to fight this thing called leukemia was ever present. I mentioned this to my wife once only to find out that she had the same feelings.

## Angel on a Bus

On this particular trip I was gone for three days. I jumped on a boat, a Carnival® ship, and I went to the Bahamas. I left on a Friday and would return that following Monday. I'll never forget we had returned to Port Miami, gotten off the boat, and now I found myself sitting in the bus waiting to be driven to the airport. I was sitting by myself only for a few minutes when this rather large woman of color moved into the seat next to me. I found myself thinking I wished they had made these seats bigger. Ignoring her, I used my cell phone to call home to check on Joshua. I had my cell phone leaning against the window so I could get better reception because the signal wasn't very strong. I called my wife and we were talking about all his blood work so while you could only hear my half of the conversation, it was obvious what we were talking about.

The conversation concerned itself with numbers and positive and negative and abnormal cells and such. So even to someone who didn't know anything about medicine, it was probably pretty obvious that we were talking about medical stuff. As with most conversations involving Joshua, I was emotional. You try to say to yourself that an emotional response here in a bus full of strangers is awkward at best, even though it didn't really bother me as much as you might think. I'm pretty secure in who I am and where I am in life. I hung up the phone with eyes glazed over and feeling that I just wanted to melt into the chair, out of sight of all these strangers. At that moment the woman reached over and put her hand on my leg. She then looked me in the eye and said with a deep southern accent, "I wasn't eavesdropping and I don't mean to pry, but I take it that you have a child that's sick?"

In a soft emotional voice I said, "Yes, that's true."

Without a hesitation she took her hand and put it over top of mine and said, "Just so you know, I said a little prayer for your child." The sincerity and love in her words truly moved me. She then said, "Now I'm going to say a little prayer for you." With that she turned away from me, closed her eyes, and with the gentleness of a butterfly moved her lips as she reached out to God for a stranger on a bus. I'll never forget that woman. I don't know her name; I only know that she was from South Carolina, but I will remember her reaching out to a total stranger and giving him comfort. I hope some day she reads this and knows in her heart that I'm talking about her. Some people believe that God places angels on earth disguised as people. If that's true, this stranger from South Carolina was surely one of God's special angels.

One thing I have always found amazing is that if you look within your life you can see God's hand in many events and circumstances. I am reminded of a time when Joshua was 12 years old. His roller hockey team was selected along with another team to play during half time at a professional roller hockey game at the Continental Arena®. This was a great honor for the children and no one appreciated it more than Joshua did.

We were getting ready to leave the house when I spied a roll of duct tape. Let me tell you, give a Ranger a knife and a roll of duct tape and he can conquer the world. Seeing the tape in the kitchen and having the helmet in my hand I figured what the heck. I tore off two pieces and placed them on the back of his helmet in the form of a cross. I figured, "Gee, it might not help, but it can't hurt."

We got to the game early and all was well. Half time came, and the kids were sent out onto the ice that had been covered so the roller hockey players could use it for their game. I should point out that this is the same arena that the New Jersey Devils® Ice Hockey team uses. Joshua was sent in. Within a few minutes was brought back to the bench and there he remained. Being the concerned parent, I rushed down to the bench and asked him why he wasn't playing. He responded, as he held his protective mask in his hand, that his face shield had broken and without it he couldn't play. He was devastated. When I asked, "Can't they fix it?" The response I got was that there weren't any tools or parts available and no time to seek them out.

I paused for a moment and then asked him to give me his helmet. As he handed it to me I know he wondered what I was going to do. I turned the helmet around removed the duct tape that I had placed just hours earlier, and using the tape repaired the faceplate. I handed the helmet back to him, told him to advise the official that the helmet was fixed, and that he could resume playing. The official on inspection of the faceplate told Joshua to take his position on the floor, and within moments Joshua scored his first goal in a professional rink.

I often wonder, "Why was the duct tape in the kitchen, why did I place the cross on the back of the helmet (never did it before), and why did the face plate break at such an important event?" All good questions. I guess some things are just left up to faith.

Joshua basically had two friends he hung out with, Ernie and Jason. They couldn't be more different. If we needed Joshua to get a little bit of that bad boy spirit in him, well, we'd send him out with Jason. Jason was good for that. Not that I'm saying Jason ever did anything wrong, but if a kid was going to do something wrong, he probably would do it while with Jason. Jason and Joshua didn't hang out a lot but there were some key times that Jason definitely contributed to making Joshua feel better about himself. Jason was a good kid, definitely full of life. I'm happy that he was around. If anybody kept Joshua thinking that tomorrow will be a better day, it definitely would be Jason. Jason had all kinds of plans for when they got their drivers' licenses. The nice thing about all these naughty ideas were that these very thoughts were the seeds of hope that we needed to plant inside Joshua.

Ernie, God blesses Ernie. Ernie was definitely Joshua's best friend. Ernie kept him company the one year he couldn't go out and has always been at Joshua's side. It was always a funny sight to see the two of them playing Nintendo wearing surgical masks because Joshua's white cell counts were way off and he couldn't have any outside exposure. Ernie would go with us to the movies occasionally. Whenever Joshua would go to the mall, Ernie would go along with him. Ernie and I had several conversations and he knew that if he observed anything that was not quite right with Joshua, no matter what he promised Joshua, he was to come to me immediately and tell me. After Joshua got sick, he was the one person we could trust to take Joshua to the mall or on trips. We knew absolutely that Ernie would take care of Joshua and not let anything happen to him.

# CHAPTER IX

# More Folks to Meet

Some of the people that had the most effect on Joshua we didn't even know all that well. On one of his trips to the local East Brunswick Mall, he and a couple of his friends got into a little pissing contest with the security guard. One of the kids was running around through an exhibit and that created a problem for the mall personnel. The security guard approached Joshua and his friends and told them they needed to knock it off. When the guard saw Joshua's hooded shirt, he started to give him a hard time about it, referring to the fact that wearing a hooded shirt made him look silly and why couldn't he be like a "normal kid" and take the hood down. What the guard didn't realize was that the chemo had taken Joshua's hair and this is how Joshua chose to hide his bald head. Joshua, of course, being your typical, arrogant teenager, told him to go screw off and he wasn't going to take off the hood. The guard's way of dealing with them was to throw him and his buddy Ernie out of the mall.

I arrived an hour later to pick them up when I noticed them waiting outside. Waiting outside is not a good thing. When I asked them why they were outside in the cold weather, they both relayed the same story. In all my dealings with people, I never remember being in a rage as much as I was then. I told them to stay in the car and I went into the mall. I approached the information desk and asked to see the highest-ranking security guard there. As I was talking, a guy about 5 feet nothing and a taller guy approached the desk and asked if anything was the matter. I turned to the shorter of the two, who was wearing lieutenant's bars, and let loose with enough raw emotion to make the devil himself back up. I told him what happened and I told him that the reason my son was wearing a hooded shirt was because he had cancer and that the chemo had taken his hair. Now, it is not my intention to make you think that this event was a pleasant exchange of words. I was yelling, using various slang terms like that SOB, come to think of it, SOB was the mildest term I used. I was angry and I wanted to hurt someone.

The supervisor said he would look into it and take the appropriate action. As I left, I spied the guilty guard pulling up to the entrance that I had just passed through. I approached his vehicle and stood in front of it and then without thinking, brought my fists down on top of its hood. I screamed at the guard to go see his supervisor. At that moment I was looking forward to him getting out of the vehicle. He didn't. I saw the other two guards coming out of the mall entrance to my rear and departed to my own car. When I got home, we told my wife the story. She didn't see it as that big a deal because the guard didn't know of all the circumstances. Joshua wanted to sue the mall. I felt the same way.

What makes this whole incident somewhat important is what happened a few days later. Joshua again went to the mall, as he did often. While he was there, this same security guard that had thrown him out just days before walked up to him, extended his hand, said he was sorry and offered any help that Joshua might need. When Joshua relayed the story to me, he dismissed it as just a series of events that happened with no more importance then that of walking out and picking up the morning paper off the driveway. I looked him in the eye and explained that for this 6 foot plus, 250 pound man to offer his hand and help was an act of courage and kindness that he should not forget for the rest of his life. When I got done talking to him I truly believe that he understood the importance of that one man's actions. I can tell you that while we may look disparagingly on most security guards, this guy won my respect and admiration. We hope today that he is well and living a good life.

Many people and places had an effect on Joshua. In Princeton I had joined a cigar club. The place was hidden inside the mall at Market Fair. Hardly anyone knew it was there and if you were not a member, you couldn't get in. Joshua had a special relationship with the folks there. Even though there were signs up that said no one under eighteen was allowed, Joshua was always welcome. We could play pool, chess, or just sit and sip brandy. Occasionally the employees would stop by to talk, which was fine to a point. On several occasions I would have to tell them that we were there for some quiet time and they would just nod and leave us to ourselves. As for the age requirement, the employees dealt with anyone who objected to Joshua being there. I never had to get involved.

When Joshua's blood work started looking real good, I took that as a sign, that we should go to Disney World®. The hospital staff took measures to ensure his safety and coordinated anything he might need with the hospital in Orlando. Everything was set for a great trip. Hey, any excuse to go to Disney World is a good excuse! We flew down on TWA® Airlines (part of Continental Airlines® now). Since we were carrying a lot of medications, syringes, and all kinds of pills and stuff, it was suggested that we let the gate personnel know what we were carrying and why. When I got to the counter, I had a letter prepared on clinic stationery that said why we were carrying all the meds and equipment. I showed it to the woman and she asked if we needed anything special, to which I responded no, I was just letting them know because it was suggested to me by the medical staff that they be aware of Joshua's condition. Well, it turned out to be a very good thing because when we got our boarding passes, we were surprised and amazed to find out that the ticket agent had moved us up to first class. Joshua really liked that. If there's anything in this world that Joshua liked, it was being treated well.

TWA treated Joshua like royalty. When we left, everyone wished him well and we were off to Disney World. Another fun day in the sun was to be had by all.

At Disney World, we stayed in Disney Village®. The first thing to do on entering the park was to stop at the Customer Service office just inside Magic Kingdom®. To find it, you enter the park and it is one of the first buildings on the left of Main Street. Joshua's doctors prepared a note explaining that Joshua should not be allowed to stand in the sun for long periods of time and anything they could do would be appreciated. The customer service girl looked over the letter and then disappeared into the back office. Several minutes later she emerged and again approached Joshua and me. She asked how many people were with the special needs person, and I told her it was just the two of us. The customer service agent then gave us special tags to carry. They're great. You don't have to wait in line. Everything at Disney World and MGM® has little side entrances that you can go through and skip the entire line process. Joshua really liked that. We saw every single event, every activity, and went on every ride we wanted to without waiting in line. We actually saw all the parks in the three days we were down there. The only difficulty we experienced during the whole trip had nothing to do with the park or its employees, but rather a fellow guest. It wasn't even a problem when you think about it.

We had decided to go over to the Jazz Club® on Pleasure Island® to have a cigar. Joshua always had time for a good cigar. Also at the time Joshua had on one of his hooded shirts. So while we were sitting there, a girl walked over. She was in her late twenties, nice looking, about five-foot-three. We're sitting at a table in front of the bar, one of those elevated types you see in a restaurant waiting area. Joshua was sitting across from me as she came up from behind me. I just nodded, said hi; she looked at Joshua smoking a cigar, noting that Joshua obviously looked like a fifteen-year-old.

She stood there firmly and says, "Is this a father and son thing?"

I was a little taken aback by it and muttered, "You mean sitting here smoking cigars?"

She responded, "Yes." She then walks closer to me: "Do you really think you should be giving him a cigar?"

I responded, "I'm his father and I thought that was my decision." So she came back expressing to me words to the effect that you should not be giving your son a cigar because he's not old enough.

Obviously irritated, I looked her in the eye and out of earshot of Joshua, I responded. Joshua knew something was going on but he wasn't sure what. He knew I would take care of it whatever it was. Looking at her and talking in a low voice, I said, "Well, he has leukemia and he has a twenty-five percent chance of not being here next year and by God, if he wants a cigar, I'm going to let him have a cigar. If you have a problem with that, that's too bad for you."

I think that got her attention because she looked up and all she said was, "Maybe I should mind my own business."

Staring now, I said, "That probably would be appropriate."

She walked away and I just turned back and faced Joshua and he said, "What did she want?"

My only response to him was, "She just had a question. No big deal." That was the end of the discussion about her and we just went on with our evening, listening to jazz and smoking some really good cigars. The whole weekend went really, really well.

We saw all the activities, we went to dinner, and he really liked the dinner at the Mexican pavilion. He wanted a margarita, alcohol and all, but that wasn't going to work out. As far as drinking, he shouldn't have any alcohol because it might have interactions with the various drugs he was taking. At home I would let him occasionally have the last ounce of beer, or a little red wine. This far from home and our usual medical support system, I was going to be overprotective. That's life. After three days, we had to go home, and of course we were flying back on TWA. Oh, we did have one last stop. The last night at Disney World I asked him where he wanted to go eat. We ended up at Hooters®.

The TWA staff asked us how the trip was. I told them it was "great," and showed them my paperwork so they knew what was going on. This return trip had a very special flight attendant named Joseph. Big, tall, black gentleman that wore a lot of gold jewelry. Again, without knowing it, they had upgraded our tickets to first class and Joseph was the flight attendant who took care of the first class section. Joseph treated Joshua like gold. Anything Joshua wanted, Joseph made sure he got it. I feel bad now because Joseph asked me if I knew the point of contact at the *Make A Wish Foundation*® because he had a niece that was seriously ill. It was his desire to get in touch with the organization. I told him I would look into it and try to find the point of contact. Joshua's wish was to be a voice in a Disney animation film. I always felt like an ass having not gotten back to him. I did fly on a TWA flight some time ago and I did have a chance to talk to some of the cabin stewards about Joseph. They knew him, so I gave him my card and asked them to express my apologies and to please have him contact me. To date, I haven't heard from Joseph. I'm hoping that if he ever reads this or someone knows him, that they pass on my name and e-mail so that he might contact me. I'm hoping that his niece has recovered from whatever her situation was. As far as TWA Airlines is concerned, I have to admit that when I fly, I still look for the cheapest tickets and whenever TWA is equal to other airlines, I always fly TWA.

Another person that played a very important role in Joshua's treatment was Donna. Donna is the mom of a girl who knew Joshua. No matter with whom I get into conversations, it's like Donna's name just never sticks. She's just always referred to as Jamie's mom. Jamie's mom is very unique. Donna has blood that is CMV negative. Now I'm not sure what all that is but I do know her blood is so good it can be given to infants. When she found out that Joshua was sick and at times needed blood transfusions, she notified the approving authority that she would withhold donating blood to anyone else just in case Joshua needed it. Donna was a regular blood donor. The problem is that if you give blood, you have to wait a certain amount of time to give again. Donna felt she couldn't take the chance of donating blood today for anyone else because Joshua might need her blood tomorrow. This came to fruition on numerous occasions when Joshua needed platelets or other blood by-products. They would call Jamie's mom and she would stop what she was doing and come down and give blood. The hospital lab would separate the parts that they needed and do whatever they do with the rest. Donna's ability to donate when Joshua needed blood was extremely important because usually at the times he needed it, we were talking a grave situation. It seemed like she always had time for Joshua.

## Another Very Special Lady

Some of my business ventures required an occasional dealing with homeowners. This one particular homeowner was a woman named V. Brooks. Mrs. Brooks is the epitome of class. If there were ever to be an ebony princess, this person would surely be the person that God intended to show up. Whenever she talked to me, it was always Mr. Laurie. It was never Jack, always Mr. Laurie. Even though occasionally I'd address her by her first name, I tried to remember to address her as Mrs. Brooks. Mrs. Brooks and I met on several occasions and as it turned out, she worked at a local college. Prior to our second meeting while going through the computer files, I happened upon the original file and on that file, it listed her husband. This was a startling thing that I noticed the name of her husband. When I discovered her husband's name, I called her office to locate her. She wasn't there but I had her cell number, so this wasn't going to hamper my efforts to locate her. I asked her secretary if she knew Mrs. Brooks well, and she said yes, she had known her for several years. I inquired, "Does her husband also work at the college?"

The secretary responded, "Yes, in fact he did work at the college but he was on a leave of absence."

I said, "Thank you," and hung up the phone and called her cell phone.

I found her driving down the road, "Hi, this is Jack Laurie."

The first thing out of her mouth was, "Hi, how are you doing today?"

I responded that I was fine and asked her how her day was going. She replied that she also was doing quite well. I told her that I had a rather large favor to ask. She said if she could, she'd be happy to do it. I said if at all possible, I would like to get a picture of her husband addressed to my son. I explained that he was sick. Her simple response was, "Well, why would you want that?"

I smiled inside and stated, "Did you think I would not recognize your husband's name?" I could picture the smile on her face. I'm sure this was not the first time this had come up in conversation with other people. She said she would see what she could do. You have to understand that this Mr. Avery Brooks is also known as Captain Sisko®, a high-ranking officer in the *Star Trek*® continuum. Several days later, when we met for the final time, she had an envelope that contained an autographed picture of her husband in character and it was addressed to my son, **"To Joshua, good luck, peace and joy. Your friend, Avery Brooks, Capt. Sisko."** When she gave me the picture, she just reached over and put her hand on my arm, and it was the gentlest of touches. She didn't really say anything. She just knew there wasn't anything to say. She's a very gracious woman. Joshua was a pretty big *Star Trek* fan. Most people would leave it at that but not her. Later Mrs. Brooks offered to make arrangements for Joshua to attend a filming of one of the *Star Trek – Deep Space 9*® episodes. The picture hangs in Joshua's room till this day, just to the left of the door as you enter.

## More Special People

Another lady that had a great impact on Joshua's life even though he didn't know it at the time was Mrs. Cipperly. I would use her first name but quite honestly I don't know it. Mrs. Cipperly was the guidance counselor at Joshua's school. She and the vice-principal of the school were the only two people in the school that knew that Joshua had leukemia. That's the way Joshua wanted it and it seemed like a pretty easy thing to honor. The biggest thing she did for us was that she ran interference without giving up his condition. This running interference was not only with the shop teacher but also with most of his other teachers as well. More about how this great lady affected Joshua's life later.

Joshua did go back to ninth grade. He missed his eighth grade in the school and had to be home tutored. Joshua went to the Vo-Tech School in East Brunswick, New Jersey. He went there because his sister went there. He just felt that it was a tradition kind of thing, besides which he really didn't want to go back to the regular school. A Vo-Tech School is an extremely wonderful opportunity for people who want something just a little bit different from a standard high school. The biggest problem we had with him going to Vo-Tech in ninth grade was that Joshua made it very clear that he didn't want anybody to know about his condition. That was a problem because Joshua missed a lot of school and some of his teachers figured he was a slacker.

One of his most important teachers and in Joshua's own mind, the most important teacher, was his shop teacher. Joshua was a welding student. Everybody called his teacher "Big Bird®." I found out the reason they called him Big Bird was because he was big and he always wore these yellow fire-retardant shirts. So Mr. Cole, the shop teacher, was dubbed "Big Bird." The guidance people were starting to hear that Joshua was not getting along with his shop teacher. It seems the shop teacher was thinking he was sloughing off and not taking things seriously because he was missing school all the time. Word was the shop teacher would do anything for a kid who put forth the effort, but a slacker received no quarter. Missing so much school gave the impression that Joshua didn't care about his studies. Teachers assumed that Joshua was skipping school. Truth is, Joshua never missed a day of school that he didn't have to miss. Even on days when he didn't go to school, many times it was under protest because we kept him home and would not allow him to go to school.

When Joshua was in the hospital, he insisted that we make up these excuses such as he was out of town, or something had come up, or that he had the flu. No one in the school system besides the vice-principal and his guidance counselor knew he had cancer. When I found out his shop teacher was not being nice and was not treating Joshua with respect, I had to meet with the guidance counselor and explain my concerns. Mrs. Cipperly said, "Things could be a lot easier if you just told him what was going on." I agreed it would make things a lot easier, but Joshua's instructions were that we not tell and at that point in time that was the deciding factor. Given those restrictions, the guidance counselor did contact Big Bird and explain to him that she could not go into details but that he needed to understand that Joshua had not cut a single day of school and at every possible opportunity was attending class. Running interference with the shop teacher was her greatest triumph. I'm not exactly sure what Big Bird thought was going on, but from then on he treated Joshua great. Joshua truly appreciated it.

Mrs. Cipperly also ran interference when it came time for gym teachers. Joshua missed a lot of gym class. Sometimes he didn't want to get dressed. The other problem was Joshua would go to school, come home, and literally crash. He wouldn't move for hours. He had just enough energy to get to school, do whatever he had to do, come home to pass out on the couch or in the bed. Also, he was playing hockey on Saturdays. There was no way we would interfere with that hockey practice. It seemed many times he lived to play hockey. So, again I had to go to Mrs. Cipperly and see if she could run some interference with the gym teachers. Eventually I went to the doctors at the clinic and said that I wanted a note to dismiss him from gym. The doctor actually started to fight me on this issue. Their original position was that if he was healthy and well enough to play roller hockey, then certainly he could take gym in school. I explained my position as Joshua's father. I made the decision that he had just enough units of energy to do the things he had to do. He did not need to participate in gym and I needed the note written. I would not categorize it as an argument. More of a discussion where both parties disagreed. But it was realized rather quickly that I wasn't backing down and the doctor did write the note which I later gave to the gym teacher.

One of the most interesting incidents that I had with people is a meeting that I planned with Joshua's teachers. Joshua's grades weren't what you would call the best grades in the world. Obviously, the fact that he missed a lot of school and he just didn't see the importance of homework and doing a lot of studying contributed to his grades not being superb. I don't begrudge him for that because in high school, I didn't do well either. It wasn't until I was a graduate student that I got the bug to learn. Then I couldn't get enough of it. I knew Joshua had the potential to be failing one or two classes. I expressed to my wife that this summer I was taking Joshua out and we were going to travel the United States. Just travel and have a lot of fun. So I called Mrs. Cipperly and asked if she could bring all his teachers together for a meeting with me. It was my intent at that meeting to tell his teachers Joshua was sick and would not be going to spend time in summer school. He was going to go out and have some fun. I didn't care if they thought he was the worst student in the world and I didn't care if they wanted to give him a "D," but given his special circumstances, failing him was not going to be a course of action that we were going to accept. In the scheme of life, giving him an "F" for a class in high school just wasn't important enough to alter the plans that I had for him. That was the original intent of the meeting as you will see later things change.

Two other people that really had a big impact on things were Ernie's mom and dad, Erin and Big Ernie. The greatest thing I can say about them is that they treated Joshua as if he were one of their own. They took him places. They made him feel like he wasn't sick. They kept tabs on him. They were good friends. We appreciated having them around. Let's also not forget the food they brought us when things got real bad. These food gifts helped us at some of our lowest moments.

# CHAPTER X

# Relapse

It was the end of April, and I had just left the office. I was riding down Route 1. It's amazing when a conversation turns to where you were when a certain event took place. The classic example, of course, being, "Where were you when JFK was shot?" I remember for that event I was in school. I wasn't particularly interested in the events of JFK's life, but it seems like you remember those kinds of things. This day I was southbound on Route 1 in New Jersey. I had just passed Ridge Road when my car phone rang. My wife was calling me and I picked up the phone and expressed the typical greeting of, "Hi, how are you? What can I do for you? I'm working." She told me to pull the car over. I knew she was at the clinic and any time she said something like that, I knew it had to be important. So I asked her, "What is it?" She said, "Pull over." I said, "I don't need to pull over. Just tell me what it is." She told me to pull over. So I pulled over into the parking lot of the Holiday Inn and I asked her what was going on. Her response was that the leukemia cells were back in Joshua's blood.

I felt like I had been kicked in the stomach by a Missouri mule when I heard those words. I asked her where she was and she responded that she was in the clinic. I said I'd be there as soon as I could. I was due to fly out that weekend for three to four days on a contract for Carnival Cruise Lines, so the first person I called was my agent. These trips generally took me rather far out of the United States. Most of the time it was in Colombia, Panama, or Costa Rica. The nearest my stage hypnosis show would have taken me was Miami or Key West. I had to call the agent and tell him that I was not going anywhere. By the time I got him on the phone, I was already crying. I explained that I was not leaving and that he needed to make other arrangements. He understood and agreed that it was appropriate to back out of the contract to take care of my son.

Within thirty minutes, I was at the clinic. It was a very somber experience when I got there. I'll never forget that Joshua was sitting in an examination room and his body language revealed that he knew he was screwed. My wife was there. I approached her and gave her a hug. Then I turned my attention to the doctor and asked, "Okay. How bad is bad?"

At that point Joshua's doctor turned to him, as she sat in the examination room, and said, "Why don't you wait outside in the hall for us?"

I couldn't have been prouder than when he looked at her and said, "Well, you can ask me to go into the hall and if you want me to, I will, but whatever you tell my dad, he's going to tell me as soon as you're done."

At which time, I looked at the doctor and said, "He's right, because whatever you tell me, I'll tell him."

She said, "Well, I guess there's no reason for him to go out into the hall, is there?" She then stated very compassionately, but very succinctly and professionally, that the arm of treatment he was on was already the most intense that they had. The relapse was significant and left no alternative as to the next course of action. We would need to get him stable and transplant him with bone marrow. She also made it very clear that at this point, things were not looking very good for him. The doctor pointed out that they were not giving up hope. We talked a little more and I asked Joshua if he had any questions. He indicated that he didn't and the doctor left the room.

After she left, I asked Joshua if he understood everything. His response was, "Basically, I figure I'm fucked."

I told him, "I don't know if you're totally screwed but things are not good." They had told us they were going to readmit him back into the hospital immediately and he would begin treatments to see if they could get him back into remission and do the transplant. I had asked the doctor if it was absolutely required that he go back to the hospital this minute or if early evening, or tomorrow morning, would be okay?" His doctor responded that it really didn't matter if it was at this very moment, but that he had to go back into the hospital tonight. I needed to go over there and get the paperwork done and get his bed set up. I told her, " fine." We went across the street from the clinic into the hospital and went back onto the children's ward, signed him in, got him a room, and then I told the nurses we were leaving.

The nurse's response to me was, "You can't leave. He needs to be admitted into the room and the work-up needs to be done!"

I looked at the duty nurse and said, "My son and I are leaving and we'll be back later."

She asked, "How much later?"

My response was simple and direct: "We'll be back when we're back." Even though I didn't share my feelings and thoughts with Joshua, I felt that once Joshua went into the hospital this time, he wasn't coming out. Sometimes you just get a feeling, and this was one of those times. People in the health profession say that a positive outlook is really important and outwardly this is what I presented. It was hard to escape the negative feelings, which consumed every fiber of my body. This unexpected relapse was not an anticipated thing, and once Joshua went back into the hospital I was sure he wasn't coming back out. If that was going to happen, if that was going to come to pass, then by God, we were going to have a nice evening.

So I grabbed him up and we got in the car. I believe he got a kick out of the fact that we were defying the hospital authorities and running away. In actuality we didn't run far. We ran to the Woodbridge Shopping Center, where there's a Ponderosa Steakhouse®. I had thought about taking him for hot dogs. Joshua had this thing about hot dogs.

Hot dogs and happiness; what a match. One of the things Joshua liked to do for late night fun was to get several hot dogs. These were not just any old hot dogs, but Gray Papaya's Hot Dogs®. So what's so good about these particular hot dogs? Well, first of all, they can only be had in New York City. Second, they were only 50 cents each. Gray Papaya's Hot Dogs are on 6th Avenue in Greenwich Village. They sell them cheap so you will also buy the fruit drinks that they sell, which is where they have a nice profit margin. Joshua didn't ever buy the fruit drinks. This was just one more way that Joshua felt like he was getting over. Our hot dog trips always started the same way. He and I would be driving around, usually in New Jersey, and I would ask him what he wanted to do.

His response would be, "What do you want to do?"

"I don't know, what do you want to do?" I would fire back.

"I don't know, what do you want to do?"

I would tell him, "Look, what the fuck do you want to do?"

He would shoot back, " I don't know, what the fuck do you want to do?"

"Look, we can't just drive around all night, so what do you want to do?"

Now with the game afoot, he would say, "Hot dogs; I want hot dogs."

Mind you the time was usually somewhere around midnight when all this would take place. So after this planned-out bantering, I would head for the New Jersey Turnpike and we would head into New York City to get hot dogs. When we arrived at the hot dog store, I would let him out with a few bucks and drive around the corner. By the time I returned, usually in no more then 10 minutes, Joshua would be waiting on the corner with a tray full of hot dogs. Sometimes we would eat them on the ride back to New Jersey, other times we would just pull forward and park the car and sit there on 6th Avenue. We would eat them while just sitting in the car; quiet time if you will. Just one of life's little simple pleasures.

For this trip I didn't feel comfortable taking him that far away from the hospital, so I hinted that Ponderosa would be a good place to eat. Joshua's favorite eating-place was the Ponderosa at the mall. Go figure. Of all the really nice restaurants we went to in New York City, Disney World, and the like, he still remained loyal to the Ponderosa at Woodbridge Mall. They had prime rib. He had prime rib at other places, but it always seemed that the prime rib there was the best. As part of the meal, they give you the salad bar and all that goes with it, such as the small pieces of chicken. Joshua would literally eat twenty-five or thirty of the chicken wings and little chicken legs. It was just his attitude that the more he ate, the more he got over on the restaurant. To him that "getting over" only enhanced the eating experience.

After dinner I took Joshua over to the jewelry store to check out the watch that I was planning on buying. I had saved for two years to get a stainless steel Rolex®. This was to be my present to me. As we stood at the counter, the saleslady pulled the watch from the display and handed it to Joshua. Joshua took the watch, and turned his head, and mimics a spitting sound, pointing his head towards the floor. "This looks cheap. Get this one." As he says this, he picks up the "Submariner®." The Submariner is the black-faced, gold-trimmed watch that has a value of almost three times as much as the stainless steel watch.

I looked at the watch he held in his hand and said, "I don't think so."

Looking at me, he gets this silly grin and says, "Look, if something happens to you, I would get the watch right? So get this one."

I thanked the saleslady and we left the store to enjoy the rest of our evening.

On our way to the restaurant, of course we had stopped and picked up some Backwoods® cigars for him and a couple of coronas (cigars, not beer) for me. We left the mall and headed to the car. Once in the car, with dinner under our belt, we opened the sunroof and just drove around for a couple of hours smoking cigars, listening to the CD player, and occasionally talking.

Mostly he just sat there and enjoyed the experience. Joshua and I could always enjoy each other's company even if nothing was ever said. There are not many people that you can just sit with and feel at ease enough to enjoy silence. As time went on, I finally called the hospital and they explained that they were having a shift change and if we didn't show up for another hour or so, it wouldn't impact anything that much. So we smoked another cigar as we went for a little ride down the Garden State Parkway and chilled out for another hour or so. The whole experience lasted about five hours. I brought him back to the hospital and signed him in. They immediately started him on some nasty chemo. I remember it was only a matter of a couple of days before he lost his hair again. The biggest thing about him losing his hair was that he didn't have hair anymore and my hair was a good half-inch long. I could actually comb my hair if I chose to. I had real hair again! I talked to my wife about Joshua losing his hair and shaving my head again. I understood that if I didn't shave my head, he'd think something was up. That negative thought process we couldn't have at this junction of his treatment. I went back to the barber. When I got to the barbershop, I explained that Joshua relapsed and that I needed him to shave it all off again. So that's what he did. When I arrived at the hospital, unlike the first time when Joshua laughed at my being bald, he didn't say a single thing. My wife said he kind of smiled. We figured that he surmised that everything would be okay because dad shaved his head. Dad would not have shaved his head if things were not looking up.

# CHAPTER XI

# The Meeting,
# Manhood, and Surprises

It was right after Joshua returned to the hospital that I remembered I had set up a meeting at the school with all his teachers for the next afternoon. This was great timing for a meeting. It was now just the day after Joshua went into the clinic and we were told that he had relapsed. I was pretty upset because Joshua had to be put back in the hospital and now the theme of the meeting had changed since he may not recover. We again had to arrange for the tutor to begin his out-of-school classes. The tutor would take over Joshua's education. The tutor at the hospital understood that she was not going to have a great deal of responsibility here because right now, the last thing we were worried about was Joshua's A, B, C's. We were trying to keep him alive. I went to Mrs. Cipperly's office. A couple of teachers had shown up and we were told that most of the teachers probably could not make it. I informed the first couple of teachers that had showed up that Joshua would be attending home schooling.

One of the teacher's responses was that home school was a joke and that the home teachers would give the student a B whether they deserved it or not. She was pretty curt about it.

All of a sudden, I'm in the guidance office with all of his teachers. Somehow their schedules had opened up. They were all in the office and they all took the attitude that they were going to help this guy straighten out his son. They were duty-bound to make sure Joshua was doing his homework and showing up for class. We were all there. I was trying to maintain. I wasn't doing a really great job of maintaining.

The more I talked, the more negative feedback was coming my way. It didn't take a genius to tell that this wasn't going over well. Finally I blurted out, "Look, you have to understand. Joshua has not missed any school because it was his choice. Joshua has leukemia and has been re-admitted into the hospital. Joshua has relapsed and we are not hopeful for the outcome."

You would think that over a period of a school year, people would figure out what was going on. What surprised me at that time was that Mrs. Cipperly and the vice-principal had been very good at their job in honoring Joshua's request that none of his teachers know he was sick. The only person that came close to knowing he was sick was his shop teacher, Big Bird®. The only thing that he knew was that there was a health issue involved and that Joshua had not deliberately skipped any of his classes. Big Bird knew there was nothing Joshua could do about it. When the teachers found out what was going on, their attitude changed and they offered some very nice suggestions about keeping him stimulated and some other things, which were very gracious. They put their hands on my shoulder and just told me to do the best I could and they were thinking of us. At this time, I didn't tell Joshua about the meeting.

During one of our many conversations, Joshua asked me to do something if things didn't work out. Joshua made me promise to deliver a bottle of vodka to Big Bird, his shop teacher. I didn't ask why. I just said I would take care of it. Another conversation we had dealt with becoming a man. Now I know that may sound silly but we had this thing going on over the years.

When Joshua was about eleven, I went to Maryland to pick his cousins up for a stay at our house in New Jersey. After I picked them up and approximately twenty minutes into the return trip, Joshua called me in the car. He told me that mommy was really sick and couldn't get out of bed all of a sudden. I talked to Pat and she said she didn't know what was wrong, but that she had to stay in bed. I again talked to Joshua and told him to keep an eye on her and to call me every twenty minutes. I also told Joshua that if he thought he needed to call an ambulance that he should just do it, and then call me. As I drove back to New Jersey, like clockwork, he called, every twenty minutes. By doing this Joshua allowed me to keep tabs on his mom. What was more remarkable was that when I got home, the kitchen, living room, and dining room were all clean. It seems that Joshua took the role of guardian to heart and made sure everything was done properly. After checking on Pat, I took him into the basement and we had a talk. I congratulated him.

He asked, "For what?"

I told him that he had just taken his first step towards manhood. Over the years, Joshua had more such experiences and shined through them. There were some family issues that came up and he handled them very well. Each time I would take him aside and tell him he took another step. When he was diagnosed, I again told him it was another step. Now with him relapsing, I again uttered those words, "Well, another step."

This time he looked at me and asked, "How many of these steps do I have to take before I am 21 years old?"

I looked him in the eye and told him, "Hate to tell you, but 21 has nothing to do with nothing. My steps took me up until I was around 31."

He looked at me in disbelief and said, "You're kidding?"

"Nope," was my response.

He just said, "Shit." I went on to tell him that at thirty-one, I finally realized that I could not make everyone like me and that was just something I had to accept.

## Stem Cells

With Joshua's new treatment getting started, the game plan was to get him to transplant. One great source of transplantable cells is what is referred to as stem cells. There are those in the medical community that believe that stem cells can be manipulated into being any kind of cell that the body might need. Stem cells for Joshua could mean the difference between life and death at this point. One of the best sources of stem cells is the blood taken from the umbilical cord of a newborn baby. As it happens, my brother Jimmy saved the umbilical blood from his twins. The lifesaving cells were currently frozen and in storage locally.

Pat and I discussed the possibility of asking for the use of the cells. With very little thought directed to the decision-making process, we both agreed that we would not ask for the cells. There is no way we were going to put Jimmy and Lorna in that kind of position. God forbid something happened to one or both of their kids. The cells would not be available because we had used them for Joshua. We never brought up the subject to anyone and kept our discussion to ourselves.

It was a matter of only a few days after Joshua was back in the hospital and Pat and I already had the discussion involving

Jimmy's archived cells that I got a call from Jimmy. I remember I was in a parking lot up on Route 15 near Sparta waiting to go to lunch when the call came in. Jimmy told me that we should have the stem cells from his kids' tested. This should be done because as cousins, they may be a match. I immediately started to cry when I heard what he was proposing. As best I could through the tears, I told him Pat and I had already dismissed using them for fear that something might happen to his children in the future. His response was that we would worry about his kids in the future, but now it was time to try to keep Joshua alive and these cells may be the means to do so. Jim and his wife Lorna had already reached an agreement to move forward and see if the cells were a match for transplant. I wonder if I could have made the same decision if it involved my kids and their possible future well being. As it was, Kristin became the donor that was the closest match. The testing process is simple, just a simple blood test, but this too had its surprises.

It wasn't long after they took the blood samples from Kristin, Pat, and me that the results were back. Pat was standing at the nurse's station when one of the medical staff approached her and said they had the results from the lab and none was a good enough match for transplant. The staff member went on further to state that Kristin and Joshua had different fathers. About the time the staff member blurted that little bit of info out, Kristin walked up. On hearing the news, she turned to her mother, and asked if that was possible. Pat's reply was a simple, "No." When Pat brought me this new information, I just laughed and told her I would have the hospital run the tests again.

The following day Pat informed a member of the medical staff that she had discussed the results with Kristin and me and that I would take care of it. This revelation startled the staff member. The medical staff person looked at Pat in amazement and fired back, "You discussed this with Kristin and Jack?"

Looking her in the eye Pat fired off, "Of course," a simple, short, bold statement.

In somewhat disbelief, her response was, "Most wives wouldn't have." It seems that this issue of different fathers comes up every so often and the medical community just tells the parents that there wasn't a good match and then leave it at that. It seems that the medical community feels it serves no purpose to tell someone that their child may not be their child.

It was later that day that I advised the staff to run the tests again, which they did. This time the tests were run at the hospital lab, and guess what? Kristin and Joshua proved to be a six-on-six match. Without belaboring the point, a six-on-six match is the best possible pairing that you can have for transplant. Oh, and by the way, it means the kids have the same father. The hospital did file a formal letter of complaint against the lab that had sent the false match report.

I guess Joshua was in the hospital about three weeks with the situation remaining bleak when my wife called me and said Joshua was having a little bit of trouble breathing. A yeast infection had set in with Joshua and he was also having trouble eating at this point. The doctors thought that yogurt couldn't hurt and it seemed like a good idea to us, too. Joshua immediately rejected the idea since he didn't particularly like the stuff. Kristin and Pat assured him that there were many different kinds of yogurt. Kristin set out to find him some yogurt that he would like.

I arrived at the hospital as quickly as I could. As I was walking down the hall, I noticed my brother, David, was there. I was actually quite relieved to see him. There's a little indentation in the wall before the clinic, which leads to the morgue. David looked at me and he didn't really say anything, but at that point, everything came home to roost. I remember collapsing in his arms and crying extremely hard. David just stood there and held me. He didn't say anything. He just held me up and told me they were going to bring Joshua out; they were moving him to intensive care. It was within minutes of losing control that I noticed the hospital staff bringing the gurney over holding Joshua.

One of the hardest things for a parent is gaining control in those times when losing control is not appropriate. It was at that point that I saw the gurney out of the corner of my eye, took a deep breath, wiped my face off, and just stood there. I had to act like nothing happened and give my feelings no more importance than dropping a bagel on the ground with the buttered side down. As they brought the gurney by with Joshua on it, David tapped him on the shoulder and said he'd see him later, wished Joshua good luck, and stated that everything would work out.

# CHAPTER XII

# Joshua Goes to ICU Again

We took Joshua up to intensive care and the big debate was whether to put him on the ventilator. It was now about an hour since the duty nurse had noticed he was having trouble breathing. His nostrils were flaring and it was evident that he was trying to get more air into his system. When we arrived at intensive care, Joshua was placed in the first bed on the left. The first thing that happened was the ICU doctors started to explain to Joshua and us what options were open to him. They're pretty good at that.

The decision was made to put him on the ventilator. So now the procedure was explained to him and at that point, Joshua felt like he had to have a bowel movement. I explained this to the nurses and they said not to worry about it, and that after they put him in a drug-induced coma, they would use a diaper system, which would not be that big a deal. I told the nurses that we were not in that much of a rush to deny him his dignity. If he wanted to use a bedpan, that's what we were going to do. The nurses responded somewhat to the effect that it would be a lot easier to clean everything up if he were put in a diaper after he was asleep. It would be much easier to work around him. I explained to them that I would take care of wiping his butt and they didn't have to worry about that. They got the message real quickly that this is something we were not going to discuss. It was a simple request, but it was important to this fifteen-year-old not to have to have a bowel movement in a diaper. Seeing my resolve, the ICU staff closed the curtain and they gave me a bedpan and toilet paper.

As it was he did try to have the bowel movement but it didn't work. The few minutes we took were just not that big a deal. At least he knew we made the effort. I could see that he was nervous and scared. The doctors then explained to him that after he was asleep, they would catheterize him. He was wondering how big the scar was going to be. Even though they were explaining to him what the procedure was, they weren't getting through to him. I asked the ICU staff to step back to give me a second. I took a piece of cardboard and drew Joshua a picture of the penis and the bladder. I showed him how the tube would be inserted. As a former military medic, I am trained in this and was pretty comfortable explaining it to him. After I explained to him what was going to be done, his anxiety settled down quite a bit. The ICU staff explained a few more things to Joshua and they asked us to go out in the waiting room where they would come and get us in a few minutes. Just before the ICU doctor put him under, Joshua asked to talk to his Oncologist. Dr. Michaels, who was already there, approached his bed. What gave Joshua the piece of mind to be placed in the coma was that he had faith in his doctor and me. Prior to being placed in the coma, he expressed to Dr. Michaels that if he was going to die anyway, he didn't need to be put in a coma, and he just wanted to be left alone. Dr. Michaels explained to him that things were not that grave yet. The most important aspect of his relationship with his doctor was his ability to rely on her to keep her promise. Dr. Michaels had told him that if things ever did get to that point, that she would come to him and explain the situation and tell him how bad things were, and she would be very honest and up front with the prognosis. This made Joshua very comfortable. I know Joshua appreciated her frankness.

We talked a few more minutes and then the ICU doctors administered the drugs to let him drift off to sleep. In my heart I knew at that point that Joshua had taken his last step towards manhood. He took charge, gave guidance, and accepted the circumstances. It's pretty remarkable for a fifteen-year-old to take his doctor aside and take charge of his life. I will never understand how people can condemn people wanting to take steps to end their own life during illness or severe injury. It seems like it's nobody else's business. Still, for a fifteen-year-old to logically and very coldly give guidance to his medical team as to what they were to do and not to do is pretty remarkable. I didn't see a fifteen-year-old boy in front of me, but a man who just hadn't realized his years yet.

At that point, my wife and I went into the little room outside the entrance to the pediatric intensive care unit to do nothing but stand and look at each other. Within a few minutes, the ICU doctors came and got us. It is an extremely emotional sight to look down and see your child hooked up with monitors and tubes coming out of him. He was intubated, catheterized, and placed in a drug-induced coma. The drug-induced coma allowed all his energies to go towards fighting the infection and his difficulty in breathing rather than being wasted on moving around or any other such thing. Also explained were the additional drugs he was to receive, particularly one such drug that worked as an amnesic. This drug was given so that when the child was removed from

ICU, he was spared the memory of his experience. When I approached Joshua's bedside, I noticed the pediatric technician was still trying to insert a nasal-gastric tube. Seeing his difficulty, I moved next to Joshua, and even though he was in a coma, I simply told him to swallow and the tube went in just fine. This was now Monday evening. We stayed for a little bit longer. We processed how long we should stay into the night. Pat went home.

I debated on going home or just going to my father's house and sleep. It served no purpose to stay in the hospital that night. After all, Joshua was in a coma and wasn't going to be moved down to the children's ward anytime soon. I thought about it and I thought about it, and I finally just came to the conclusion that if I had to think about it that much, I must know deep down inside I needed to stay. I had promised him a long time ago that he would never be in the hospital alone. Now was not the time to break my word. The nurses were really great down in PEDHEMOC. They set me up a bed in the conference room of the Pediatric-Hematology-Oncology unit itself with the stipulation that I understood that come nine o'clock in the morning, I had to be out of there. They would need the room. So I slept that night, Monday night, in the hospital. Next morning when I got up, I spent time with Joshua and things were not going great, but they weren't bad either. One of the interesting things was when the ICU doctor gave us our briefing on Monday night, she told us that Joshua was stable and she was going to go home. She said that a lot of parents were concerned that the doctor in charge would be leaving the unit for the night. Noticing our discomfort, she added that it was a very good thing, because if she was allowed to go home, it meant that everything was stable and there was no crisis situation. So if people called up to talk to her and she was not there, that was actually a good thing because it meant that things weren't as bad as they could be.

The following night I again spent the night in the hospital. During the day, I spent as much time as I could with Joshua. I wasn't getting a lot of work done. Pat soon came to the hospital with Kristin. There was not much, really, you could do. You could sit there. You could sit there and cry. I remembered back to just before he was placed in this drug-induced coma. Joshua talked to his doctor, his oncologist, and explained to her that if things were not going well, she was to stop all treatment. This memory sparked an older one. I remember at one point at least some six months earlier, my wife wanted Joshua to go to confirmation class and Joshua's response was that he did not want to go. Pat and Joshua got into a little bit of an argument. Finally she came to me under the guise of "When your father gets home..." She said that I needed to go talk to my son and make him understand that he had to go to confirmation class. She fully expected me to be her ally in this. My response to her was just the opposite. I remember telling her, "If you were taking him to church to give him a better understanding of God, I don't see how that's possible." Joshua had long determined before he was in intensive care that he believed eventually, he was going to die from his illness, and he was comfortable with that. The fact that he was comfortable and ready to die and go meet God made me think that going to church one or two more times was not going to clarify his thinking. Joshua already had an understanding of God, and his faith was strong. I don't think he needed to go to church. If the only reason he's going to church is to get a better understanding of God and the whole concept of heaven and hell, well, I think for a fifteen-year-old, he had it. As a fifteen-year-old facing what he believes will eventually be death, he has a pretty clear understanding of it. It would be inappropriate for me as his father to tell him he had to go to church. Pat thought about it a little bit and I don't know if she totally agreed with me or not, but the end result was that he didn't go to confirmation class.

The night he was admitted, Monday night, when we sat down with the doctors and they were explaining what they were going to do, without bearing any names, I asked everybody in the room to leave except the one doctor. I wanted to have an open, honest discussion with this doctor. I didn't want anybody else around so there wouldn't be a discussion later about who said what. It was simply a matter of one person talking to another person. I asked this particular doctor, "With regard to Joshua's wishes, if things are not going well, what would be the logistics of how things would be handled?" The doctor explained that they would honor his wishes and explained the various avenues of approach that someone might take given situation A, B, or C.

I spent Tuesday night sleeping in the conference room again. Tuesday was a hard day. In the morning all I could do was sit next to Joshua and cry. His doctors came by and all they saw was a dad with water running down his face as if he were standing in a shower. They didn't say anything; just reached over and said hello. Nothing remarkable was taking place. Joshua just lay there and it seemed that they were putting drugs into him every few minutes.

As I was sitting there next to him, with all those tubes coming out of him, I felt like my world was compressing in on my head. There was not much I could do but sit there, and think about everything, from paying my rent, to what am I going to tell people if this phase of his treatment doesn't work. I reminded myself, that the most important thing was to be there, and be accountable only to him.

Just a few nights ago, Joshua and I got into an argument. As before, when he got really angry he would yell, "You know I didn't ask you to stay up here." That was his line when he was really mad. But, he never followed up with, "You can go home," or "I don't need you here." So like several times before, I just ignored his banter, watched TV, and laid down knowing that sooner or later he would want to talk.

It was about midnight when I heard his shallow voice, "Dad, If I need help tonight will you help me?"

I looked up from my small bed in the corner and told him, "When you need me I will always be here." A little while later the chemo kicked in, and in his using the bathroom things got a little messy. So between the two of us, it took a few minutes to clean him up. Later on that night, when he thought I was asleep, he did his little thing of sitting up, and checking to see if I was still there. He is still a little boy, despite his courage, and his maturity. I don't think Joshua feared dying, as much as he feared being helpless.

Wednesday morning came early and things were not going well. Joshua's oxygenation process was really getting bad. That's when the doctors called Pat, Kristin, and me into the small conference room next to the ICU. The doctors sat us down and began to explain that things were not going good and they said they had to do a procedure by which they were going to insert a catheter into Joshua's heart and lungs. The procedure itself could be life threatening and that it needed to be done because they were trying to determine which course of drug therapy to take. One drug therapy would be good for his heart but bad for his lungs. The other therapy would be good for his lungs and bad for his heart. The only way to determine which one to take was to insert a catheter and take various measurements once inside Joshua's body. The ICU doctor very calmly and very professionally, extremely professionally, explained that things were not going well and Joshua was now in a life-threatening situation. I explained to the ICU doctor Joshua's wishes about how far treatment was to go and we talked about the various things we would and would not do. The catheter insertion, at times, could cause cardiac arrest. It was determined that at that time if the cardiac arrest would come about, that the ICU staff would take action to re-start the heart. This heart stoppage was viewed not as a termination of life necessarily but as a side effect of the procedure. This was not an extraordinary means for keeping Joshua alive. Resuscitating was just simply a reaction to a heart stoppage because of the procedure.

The ICU doctor also understood that if the procedure was over and cardiac arrest came about, that under certain criteria, they would not resuscitate. We talked for a few minutes and at that point, it was obvious that things were not going well and I had strong concerns that Joshua was not going to survive the procedure, let alone a few more days in intensive care. I informed the ICU doctor that before anything was going to be done that he was to call this one particular oncologist (Dr. Michaels) that Joshua had given guidance to and she was to come to the intensive care unit. The ICU doctor explained to me that this wasn't necessary. I am always amazed at what doctors think is and is not necessary. This is not a put-down; this is simply a statement as a perception. I informed the ICU doctor that there was going to be no procedure until this particular oncologist got up to the wing. He agreed and Joshua's oncologist was called. When Dr. Michaels arrived, I looked at her and

I explained that they wanted to do this procedure and she already knew because they had contacted her earlier. I told her that this is a situation now that Joshua might not survive or extraordinary measures might become necessary very quickly to keep him alive. It was time for her to live up to her promise in explaining how things might develop. I knew Joshua relied on me to honor his wishes. I looked at her and said, "You need to go talk to Joshua." Her response was that he was in a coma and he may or may not hear her. She stated if that's what I wanted done, that's what she would do. I explained that what I wanted had nothing to do with anything at this point. What I wanted was my son going to the mall, going to college, having a family, and enjoying sunsets and sunrises. In my heart I knew none of this was likely to happen.

It was now twelve o'clock and Pat, Kristin, and I were in the Intensive Care Unit. Another visitor had shown up as well, Pastor Schott. Pastor Schott had arrived just for a simple visit, just a pop in to say hi and see how things were going. What he had in fact walked in on caught him off guard, and a situation that was totally unexpected. As we all stood there, Dr. Michaels leaned over to Joshua and positioned her face right next to his left ear. I was in a position that I could hear most of what she was telling him. Dr. Michaels was explaining how serious things were, what they were trying to do for him, things were not looking real, real good, further, they were going to try everything they could and that she would take care of him. The conversation with him lasted about six to eight minutes. When Dr. Michaels was done talking with Joshua, the intensive care doctor traded places with her and leaned over in the same manner and started to explain to Joshua what was going to be done. No one will ever convince me that someone in a coma cannot hear. As soon as the ICU doctor started to explain the procedure, everything started to crash. Joshua was not having it. Immediately everything started to shut down. I watched the monitors as the blood pressure started to crash. This all took place within seconds of the ICU doctor talking to him. As Joshua started to crash, the intensive care doctor instructed the nurse to take the three of us out of ICU.

At first the three of us just stood outside the doors to the Intensive Care Unit. We could hear things as they were progressing, and Christine (Thanatologist or grief counselor) had to restrain Kristin from going back into the ward. I was happy to let her perform this function as I just stood there and tried to contemplate what was going on. In a matter of moments, the decision was made to move us over to a room that they had hastily set up. There was a room just outside of the wing that was obviously used to hold infants. There were cradles lined up against the wall. It was a small room that felt very crowded. Pat, Kristin, and I, along with the pastor from my wife's church and the Catholic priest from the hospital's church, just sat there. It was a very emotional time. I remember getting up and walking around. I remember hitting the wall with my open hand and I made some comment that this just wasn't fair. I remember crying.

Then I remember sitting down and it's almost to the point where I felt comical thinking out loud. I said, "If just the nurse comes in, we know things aren't as bad as what we think." I then added, "If Joshua's oncologist comes in, then we know that things are worse but we're not in dire straits. If the Intensive Care doctor comes in, then basically we know we are screwed." It wasn't ten seconds after I finished saying those three things to those people in the room that in walked the nurse, the oncologist, the Intensive Care doctor, and Christine, the grief counselor. The Intensive Care doctor took charge of the room.

He sat down and he looked as if somebody had just run over his favorite puppy. He was visibly upset. He explained that they hadn't even started the procedure they were going to do because essentially there was no need to. He explained that they had done all that they could at that point. He looked up again and said that he had done all he could do. Now what Joshua needed was his family, not him.

One of the things that parents have to deal with is the appropriate reaction at the appropriate time. It's the simple things. I remember when I was eating nacho chips and Joshua had to throw up. I knew if I reacted to him throwing up it would only make things worse for him. The whole point being that if you're upset, the child gets more upset. So we're sitting in a hospital room and I'm holding this bucket and in one hand intertwined with my fingers I'm holding a bag of chips. With the other hand I'm removing chips and eating them as his guts are emptying into the bucket. As bad as you want to throw up with your child, that just makes them more upset, so what you have to do is ignore it like it's an everyday, simple activity. Well, now I had to go into the room and essentially send my son to God. It was time to honor promise number two. Long ago I had promised him that if things didn't work out, I would not let him die alone. That I would hold him and he wasn't to be afraid. When it came to Joshua, he needed me to be there and any petty excuse that it would be too emotional was just not going to happen. I was not letting my son die alone. No matter how much it would be uncomfortable for me, that's probably the ultimate responsibility of a parent. It's probably one of the hardest and yet easiest responsibilities of a parent to hold a child while he dies. There was never any doubt in my mind as to how we would handle his passing. We went into the Intensive Care Unit.

There were nurses and doctors all around him. Pat positioned herself on his left side down by his waist/thigh area and held his hand. Kristin was down on the right side of the bed by his foot. I was at the head of the bed and cradled Joshua's head in my arms. As I cradled him in my arms, I told him it was time to let go and that he should go to God. I explained to him that we loved him and we would miss him. That when he got to heaven, his dogs Pepsee and Smooch would be there waiting for him, and that it was time to go. I remember telling him to just let it go, let it go. The ironic thing about that phrase was that when I do hypnosis shows and I want people to de-stress, one of the phrases I always use for them is, "Take a deep breath now and just let it go. Let it go."

I was watching the nurses out of the corner of my eye. They were still administering drugs to his I.V. line. At the time I honestly don't know if the drugs were to make his passing easier or for our benefit to keep him alive. I later learned they were giving him pain meds to prevent his having any discomfort at the end. At one o'clock, Joshua died. Present when he died was his mother, his sister, and me, the Catholic priest from the hospital, Pastor Schott, all four of his oncologists, ICU doctors, nurses, and Christine. As I had promised him, he did not die alone. They turned the monitors off while we were there but you could tell by looking at him and you could hear the alarm that went off at the main station that it was over. Pat and I understood what was happening.

The ICU medical staff asked us to step back and the ICU doctor, utilizing his stethoscope, determined that Joshua had died. The attending doctor turned off the respirator and other equipment. This action startled Kristin. She didn't seem to understand what was going on and wanted to know why the doctor was putting his hands on Joshua. This was a very intense thing for her. I don't think Kristin was ready to give up the role of protector yet. In the past, as early as when she was four, she had looked out for Joshua. The first time she was trying to hold him back when he was just learning to use his walker. He was moving towards a fan we had placed on the floor. Kristin was holding him back with all her strength and screaming for help. Years later when she was around six, Joshua was riding his Hot Wheels® tricycle. He had crossed into the street in front of the house. This time a guy came driving down the street. As he started to speed up, he noticed a little girl deliberately riding into the street, blocking his path. We could see his face as he cursed and berated the child until she moved her bike. At that moment he noticed the small boy just a few inches off the ground that he would have hit had he not stopped. Joshua didn't need a guardian angel; he had Kristin.

The ICU doctor moved away from the bed and told us that it was over. I asked him to remove the tubes. He said they'd be happy to do it, but that I should understand that sometimes it is a messy procedure because of the material in the patient's stomach. My response was to just leave everything the way it is. They made no rush to do anything at that point. The ICU staff was very respectful about the situation. Very mindful about what was happening.

After a minute or two, I looked at my wife and said, "Should we leave?" She said she wasn't ready yet, but that I could. Christine, seeing me start to leave, inquired of Pat if I should be alone. Pat indicated that might not be a good thing, at which point Dr. Michaels grabbed me up and we went for a walk. Pat's only guidance was that I was not to make any phone calls just yet. Side by side, Dr. Michaels and I walked about the hospital floor talking of Joshua. I remarked that I guess he heard her when she told him how bad things were. Dr. Michaels said Joshua either shut down or it was the strongest case of coincidence that she had seen in her entire life. I came back with the comment that I guess he had had enough. We talked further, about the weather, about things. I was pretty self-centered at that point. After a small amount of time passed, I returned to Joshua's bedside. At this point Kristin left and went with Christine, and I was at a loss as to what to do. I asked Pat again if we should leave. She said if I wanted to that was okay but that she was going to stay awhile longer.

I turned and walked to the other side of the curtain that the ICU staff had placed around the bed. I knew what my next duty was. I stepped outside the curtain and some of the staff made a move to go into the curtained area. Mind you there was no meaning of intrusion on their part, but I put out my hand, then crossed my arms and there were no words spoken. My meaning required no further explanation; no one was to enter the bed area until Pat was done.

I stood and talked to the doctors and a few others. No one moved to enter the bed area. I just stood there at the entrance of the curtained area with my hands crossed and my feet shoulder-width apart, not really keeping track of time. I was really trying not to be an imposing figure. At the same time I was trying to give the impression that at this point in time, nobody was entering the curtained area until Pat said it was okay. I hesitate to use the phrase, "I stood there guarding the entrance," but basically that's what I did.

Everybody respected that and nobody made a move towards the curtained area. I believe that I stood there for between 15 and 20 minutes. To tell the truth, I'm not sure how long it was. Then Pat gave an indication that it was fine now and if somebody needed to come into the area, that would be okay. By now Kristin had joined Pat at Joshua's side, while at the same time I approached Dr. Michaels concerning an autopsy. I made comments to the effect that parents shouldn't have to go through this and that they had my permission to take whatever tissue samples they needed.

We moved over to the side area of the monitoring desk and I signed a release to perform whatever tests they deemed appropriate with the one stipulation that his head was not to be touched. I'm not sure why I said that other than the fact that there would be certain people that would want to see him before he was laid to rest and I didn't want any kind of scarring or marks on his face. Dr. Michaels explained there were no tissue samples that would be needed from the head area and that would be a very easy request to honor. I signed the papers and at that point, I really don't know what happened in Intensive Care.

Before I left the hospital, I had a chance to talk to Pastor Schott. Pastor Schott is an interesting guy. He had just come up to see Joshua to say hi. He didn't know what he was walking into. He made the remark that he was impressed at the way things were handled. He felt that he would carry the experience with him for a long time. Pastor Schott actually thanked us for allowing him to be part of the experience. I believe that Joshua's short life contributed greatly to the universal experience, and that his life experiences will go on and be used by and for others in their own endeavors. Even in death, Joshua was a great contributor to the world's scheme of things.

The only thing I knew is that I had one more thing to do. It was about one-thirty or so in the afternoon and I expressed to my wife that I had to go and buy a bottle of vodka. Prior to leaving the hospital, I knew I had to go down and clear my stuff out of **The Room**; last trip. I remember walking through the door and that's the first time I used that phrase, "Things didn't work out." Brandy's mom was playing with Brandy over in the toy area. Brandy was a little baby about 19 months old and had cancer. On several occasions I had helped Brandy's mom feed her. She looked up at me and asked how things were going. I told her that it didn't work out. I didn't know at that point that she didn't know what I was talking about. It was only later that she found out that Joshua died and understood (Brandy died a few months later).

As I approached Joshua's old room, somebody had already been put in it. As I stood there, one of the nurses approached me and very curtly asked me what I was doing. I think my actions of approaching the room with another patient in it caught her off guard. I turned to her and said I wasn't doing anything. I was just looking at the room and the nurse looked at me. That's when I turned to her and I said that for Joshua, it didn't work out. She immediately started to cry. I remember wrapping my arms around her and just holding her. You would think that they would be used to dealing with children that had life threatening illnesses dying. I guess this one nurse hadn't gotten the hang of watching kids die yet. She was quite upset. I held her for a couple of minutes. Other nurses in the unit were visibly upset because they hadn't gotten the word yet that Joshua had died until I blurted it out. After I let her go, I had to get my stuff out of the conference room. I threw everything in some big bags. My final act that I performed at the clinic was to give a twenty-year-old girl my air mattress that I had been sleeping on over the last nineteen months. Whenever she stayed in the hospital, her mom would stay over too. I gave her my air mattress and wished her good luck. I also took a few moments to explain the best way to make the fold down chair into a bed, and then I left. I hope she made it.

# CHAPTER XIII

# Telling Others

After Joshua died and we left the hospital, it was time to start telling people what happened. That was not going to be a fun experience by any means. My wife offered to tell my family members that things were now over and Joshua had died. She's very strong in that way.

Pat always was the stronger of the two of us. There's no getting around it; there's no denying it. I accept it for what it is. I don't see it as a weakness on my part. It is just the way that it is; I accept that. As I said, she offered to tell my parents and my brothers. We had some discussion along those lines but the basic premise was that it was my responsibility because it was my family.

I remember driving over to my father's house thinking this was going to be an emotional roller coaster. I knocked on the door. They always kept it locked. I entered the house and as I entered the house, my father was coming out of the kitchen. The kitchen is adjacent to the rear of the living room. As he entered the living room, I reached around him and I grabbed him in a bear hug fashion. As I did that, I noticed my mother was standing to my left, her hand was on the back of my father's favorite reading chair. As I held my father, I whispered in his ear that it was over—one of two phrases that I would use a lot over the next few days. The other phrase would be, "Things didn't work out." Very simple words, but very powerful nonetheless. When I whispered in my father's ear that it was over, he immediately started crying. I don't know if my mother overheard or not but it was obvious that she understood what I had just conveyed. I reached out with my left arm and she approached us and the three of us just stood there. As I held them in my arms, they said words to the effect of, "Oh, no. My God," another simple phrase that really means nothing and means everything. After a few moments, they just cried.

After a time, my mother sat on the couch and my father sat in the chair she had been leaning on when I first came in. I tried to—as stoically as I could—explain the events of the last few hours. I think I take my emotionalism from my father. He just sat in the chair and looked old. At one point, he hammered his hands on the chair arms and stomped his feet as a small child would if they were having a tantrum, just shaking his head, screaming, "No, no, no." I went over to him and put my hand on him and he just leaned over and cried. It was at that point that he stated that Joshua would have a coffin. "He was a good little Jewish boy. He has to be buried in a Jewish coffin." At the time I had no idea what he was talking about but I would learn later at the funeral home, it's a very simple coffin, no nails. Everything is glued together. Everything is made by hand. As a last request for his grandson, his first grandson, it seemed like a very simple thing to honor.

Next, phone calls had to be made. The first one was to my brother Jimmy. I caught Jimmy riding down Route 1, of all places. Route 1 was the same highway I was on when I got the call that Joshua had relapsed. I asked him who was driving and as soon as I said that, he knew something was up. It's amazing that people will say things like sit down or are you alone or where are you and the person that's receiving that message knows something is going on and that most likely, it's not a good thing. Jimmy responded that he wasn't driving and asked what was going on.

I said, "Why don't you stop the truck?"

With impatience in his voice, he said, "I don't need to stop the truck. What's going on?" I expressed to him that it was over. He didn't quite understand right off the bat what I was talking about. I had to get a little descriptive. I told him that at one o'clock Joshua had died. He immediately started to cry. Jimmy, before, during and after Joshua's death, has always been a very emotional person. He said he would be over in a matter of minutes. Subsequent to that, it was no more than ten or fifteen minutes and we greeted him and just hugged him and he just cried some more. My mother held him. I let her take over consoling him. At that point, I think I was being a little selfish and trying to figure out how I was going to tell my other brothers what had happened.

I had a million things on my mind and was happy to let my mother deal with Jimmy. Then I had to find David. David was at a local gym somewhere. Jimmy knew he was at a gym but he didn't know where. So we called around and found someone who knew David and what gym he would be at. We called the gym and got a guy on the phone that knew David. We expressed to that particular individual that we needed to talk to David rather quickly and that there was a family thing happening and he wasn't to say a word to David. All he was to do was get him to the phone. David came to the phone and I remember telling him that at one o'clock Joshua had died. Our conversation was very short. He said he'd be right over and within 30 minutes he arrived at my parents' house. As with most of my family, he was visibly upset. I'm not sure David ever realized that he was the last of my family to ever see Joshua alive. When he told him to hang in there at the hospital, that was the last time anyone from the immediate family other than Pat, Kristin, and myself saw him alive.

The next call I had to make was to my brother Ricky, in California. I remember expressing to my wife that we were now going to have to make arrangements for a funeral and it really made no sense for Ricky to come all the way over from California to New Jersey. Him being there or not being there was not going to change the fact that Joshua had died. He didn't need to go through that kind of expense. It's remarkable that my wife's response to that was she was sure that once I told Ricky that Joshua had died, he'd be on the next plane. I remember saying, "Well, we'll see, but he really doesn't need to do that."

Pat said, "You wait and see. I'm telling you that as soon as you tell him, he's going to be on his way home." I learned long ago not to question Pat's insights.

Ricky was call number three. I called him in his office; he was having some kind of meeting. I remember him asking very happily as a brother would say to another brother, "How's it going?" I told him that I just came from the hospital and it was over. I really didn't have to elaborate to him. He understood immediately what I meant and he began to cry. If the people were in his office, I'm sure they left the room. Rick's immediate response was, he'd make arrangements to get home as quickly as possible. I remember thinking that's what Pat said he'd do. I never expressed to him that he didn't need to come home. The truth of it was, I was glad to have him there.

It seems for all the important events in my family, everybody attends. I remember years prior, they had a family reunion and the various families involved had several children and grandchildren and cousins and aunts and everything. But the one thing that's unique with the Laurie Family is that when we showed up at the reunion, it was my mother and father and all four boys. No other family at the reunion had everybody there. To tell Ricky not to come home just seemed like the furthest thing from my mind. It really never came up. I remember hanging up the phone and telling my parents that Ricky would be home soon. Within a matter of hours, Rick called back and said he was going to get a flight the next day. For those of you that don't know, airlines offer discounts for situations like this. I honestly don't know if my brother got a discount or not. It just never came up. I do know if you tell an airline there's been a death in the family, many of the airlines will offer you, if not a discounted ticket, a ticket at a cost that is much less than what a last minute ticket would cost. Rick showed up at our house the next day. I could hear him approaching the front door. It was like a rerun of my approaching my father's house twentyone months ago when I had to broach the subject of Joshua's leukemia for the first time with my parents. With every step he took, approaching the door, I could hear him sobbing louder. Pat met him at the door and just held onto him and brought him in. We sat by each other for awhile before we talked. Rick didn't understand any better than the rest of us. Every step of the way, Joshua had looked so good. Just before he relapsed, he had gone to a wedding. He was all dressed up and ready to make his mark on the world. He wore a suit with a red tie. While he did take the jacket off, he never did loosen his tie like everyone else. I guess he figured if your going to dress the part, you have to dress it right.

When it came time to notify other people that Joshua had died, I mostly bowed out. Pat and Kristin notified more people than I ever would have. My primary duty was to tell my family. As a secondary thing, there were several other people that I saw as my responsibility to tell, and those I did.

I had one more stop that I had to make. I'm not sure what liquor store I used but I remember stopping in East Brunswick. As I entered the store, I asked the clerk what was the best vodka they had. The clerk pointed out a bottle of "Gray Goose®." I thanked him, paid for the bottle, and exited the store.

While I was driving, I remembered a call that I felt I needed to make. Notifying one more person wasn't going to kill me, and I felt the news should come from me. I needed to let Pearl know what had happened. The way I did it was kind of wimpish. I called Pearl's computer store and asked to talk to Pat, her husband. I got the office manager and told her who I was and that I needed Pat paged, and a return call as soon as possible. I stressed to the manager that it was important. Within a few minutes, Pat called me on my cell phone and asked what was up. I told him of the events of the last few hours and asked him to tell Pearl. I expressed to him that I just couldn't tell one more emotional person today. Pat understood and said he would take care of it.

Just as the phone conversation with Pearl's husband ended, I arrived at Joshua's school. I took the vodka from the passenger seat in the car and entered the school building. I set out to find Joshua's welding shop teacher. That was one of those events that will be remembered for a long time. It was around three o'clock when I arrived at the school. At the time I didn't know it but Kristin was also at Joshua's school. Kristin had stopped in the office to talk to the guidance folks, but the person I needed was Joshua's shop teacher. Joshua had taken welding and re-ally liked it. His shop teacher was real important to him. The guy was a good egg. I ran into Big Bird® in the back hall area. He had just come out of class. He greeted me and we started to talk. He said he had seen Kristin and asked how Joshua was. I looked at him and asked when he had seen Kristin. He replied, "Just yesterday." I looked at him and as calmly as I could, told him that Joshua had died at 1:00 p.m. He was visibly upset. I then told him that the last thing I had promised to do for Joshua was that if it didn't work out, I was to deliver this bottle of vodka to him. With that, I handed him the vodka. His response was one of astonishment and great sadness. He asked me why, and I responded I didn't know and I hadn't asked Joshua. Big Bird said that night he would drink it and toast Joshua. With the delivery of the vodka, I fulfilled my third and last promise to my son.

I had to stop at work for some things and there, as always, was Ann Marie holding down the fort. I would like to say, for the record, thank God for her. She kept everything running these many last months. Without her the business would have floundered, and there is no telling how much effort it would have taken to get it back on course. When I got to the office, I told her it was over and she immediately became upset. She gave me a hug, and asked if there was anything that she could do. I told her no and that she could leave for the day anytime she wanted. I didn't stay for more than a minute and then I headed home.

By the time I got home, Pat and Kristin were already there. Once I had gotten home, it was pretty non-stop on the phone. Kristin took care of most of it. There were people we knew that were going to come over. It's not my goal or desire to leave anybody out. It's just that there were so many. Erin came over almost immediately. She was very, very upset. Later on at night, a friend of mine, Tommy, would come over.

One of the people I knew would eventually come over was Loretta. Loretta and David had lost their child years prior to this. I remember going to the funeral and there's something about a child dying that's very emotional. Loretta arrived the following day. I was getting into my car and I looked up and saw this car pull up and I didn't recognize the car and sure enough, out steps Loretta. Almost immediately after she got out of the car, she started to cry. Of course once she started to cry, I started to cry. We just held onto each other for a few moments. It was comforting to know that this was the one friend out of all the people that we knew who understood what we were going through. I felt bad for her about the way she found out. Tom and Diane's daughter, Kelly, is a very close friend of the family and particularly of Kristin. Tom and Diane's children are considered cousins to my kids even though there's no biological relationship. It's just that they have known each other for so long, we're pretty much considered aunt and uncle. It was just one of those long-term friend kind of things. To describe it, where you look at somebody as more than a friend, even though you're not really a family member. Loretta had bumped into Kelly's husband at the local food store and she had greeted him, "Hi, how are things going?" His response was that Kelly was upset because her cousin had died. Loretta replied that she didn't know any of Kelly's cousins were sick, to which he responded that her cousin had leukemia. Well, she knew at that point whom he was talking about. It was then that she immediately exited the store and came to the house. Loretta and I talked for awhile and then I had to leave. As I pulled away from the house, I saw her walking towards Pat, who by now had come outside when she saw what was happening. A few hours later, I was home and somebody came knocking at the door and of course, it was Loretta's husband, David. We sat on the front porch and talked for a little bit. He gave me the standard line that things really suck right now but eventually they, get better. Then he told me about a group called Compassionate Friends®. It was a support group for parents who lost children or some other significant person. We just sat there and he saw no need to say anything more. We talked about Joshua. We talked about the weather. We just talked about things.

One of the persons that it was my responsibility to tell that Joshua had passed was Toby. Toby was the video guy. Toby had made an extra effort to make sure Joshua always had videos and always got the new releases a day earlier than everybody else. That became extremely important to Joshua. It was all these little things that made life a little easier. So it was my responsibility to tell Toby. I found Toby in the video store and told him what had happened and thanked him for everything. He asked if he could do anything, and I just said thanks and left the store. I still see him around town and I still think of him as a great guy.

The only other person outside of the family that I saw as my responsibility to tell was Mrs. Brooks. I had already told others as various situations and opportunities presented themselves. I knew there was one person that I had to deliberately seek out and tell. I would have to be the one to tell Mrs. Brooks. Her kindness necessitated at least a personal phone call, and most likely more. She had offered to arrange a tour of the studio where her husband worked. This offer was not a trivial thing. I felt it was extremely important to notify her that this was not going to happen, and that we were extremely grateful that she had gone through all the efforts on his behalf. That was going to be a very hard conversation to have. The biggest thing I remember about the conversation was no matter how hard I tried to stay calm while talking to her, it wasn't two seconds into the conversation that she realized something was wrong and she told me to take a deep breath and tell her what was wrong. Mrs. Brooks was pretty insightful for someone with whom I had limited contact. I know I will always remember her. It would be pretty hard to forget her. She is one classy lady. She asked where the services would be and I told her the little I knew.

# CHAPTER XIV

# Setting Things in Motion

The next big milestone was going to be the funeral arrangements. For someone with no experience on how to arrange a funeral, the only thing I could think to do was seek out my parents' advice. At least they knew who to call. We used a place called Gleason's Funeral Home®. I'm not sure why we used Gleason's. When I was in high school, the school bus went by Gleason's Funeral Home every day. It was a landmark in Franklin Township, where I grew up. Nobody said anything bad about him. I didn't know anything good about him, but nobody said anything bad about him. So I contacted them and we made arrangements to go over there and talk. When my wife, Kristin, and I arrived, I had expressed that my father's request was that Joshua be buried in a Jewish casket. We had already determined that we were going to have Joshua cremated, so this request was pretty simple to honor. The lady we were talking to knew right away what my father had been talking about. She showed us various pictures of coffins and explained the significance of each. That made my decision-making process very simple. I said, "Give me the simplest and most plain casket that they make." As the custom was explained to me, this is the way it had to be. The whole idea behind the coffin was that you appear humble before God when you get to heaven.

My daughter expressed a difference of opinion here and my wife said I wasn't taking Kristin's needs into consideration. Of course she was right but I had made up my mind on this point and I saw no reason to change it. I was getting a little bit self-centered again and arrogant, but this was the only request my father had made of me. I told the funeral director I wanted the simplest, plainest Jewish coffin that they made. My daughter expressed some desire for a little more fancy coffin, and I don't begrudge her that. I just said no. There was no chance I was changing my mind. So I brought the discussion making to a halt. One of the premises I expressed to my wife was Joshua was my son and this is how it was being done; this is what we were going to do. Of all the things that I handled right, the whole business of the coffin could have been handled better. I could chalk it up to stress, arrogance, or just plain being an ass, but I could have handled it better; sorry. One thing nice about the funeral home was that they expressed that they knew how devastating it was to lose a child and they immediately cut the price in half. At the time, I felt that was a really good sales pitch.

Foolish me, later I would learn that when it comes to the expense of burying a person, they did in fact cut the fee in half. Given the financial resources we had at the time, that was greatly appreciated. We never did seek a second opinion on how to handle things. I don't know if people do want to get second opinions on funeral arrangements. It's not like you're putting in a pool and you get five contractors out there and you discuss it and weigh the pros and cons of each one and then decide who you're going to choose. We had come to the funeral home and they told us how everything is done. They would notify the newspapers, set up the service and walk us through step by step. There was no discussion on should we go somewhere else. The funeral home staff did express to us that when it came to children, there tends to be more people than you anticipate. I didn't really think that was true. When it came time for the service, we had three hundred plus people show up. Joshua had a remarkable impact on many people's lives.

I should point out that I would never tell anyone how to handle the passing of a loved one. On the day we held the funeral service for Joshua, Pat and I both worked. For me it just seemed the natural thing to do. Pat had shipping orders to process, and if she didn't do it today, she would just have to do it tomorrow. The only difference then would be that instead of UPS® delivering the items, I would likely have to deliver them myself. She didn't have time to finish one order, so she called the dealer and advised them that we would only be sending half the order today and the rest would follow tomorrow. The dealer advised Pat that they preferred the whole order be sent right then. She then had to tell them that she had to attend the funeral service for our son and that the rest would have to go out tomorrow. On hearing that, the dealer agreed that it would be okay. Pat never liked to talk to strangers about personal things.

I was amazed at how many people actually read the obituary section of the newspaper because just as the funeral director had said, there was a tremendous amount of people that showed up. When it came time for Joshua's funeral, they had a room where the casket was laid out and the funeral staff actually had to open up the entire front of the building. Making the viewing area larger was done by opening a wall that separated the two viewing areas at the front of the building. Now the viewing area was made into one large room. This extends the service area into the entire length of the building. Pastor Schott honored us by conducting the service. It was a rather interesting service because we had a Lutheran pastor conducting with a very strong Jewish overtone. After the service I handed Pastor Schott a check with the payee left out. I felt he could write in whatever he wanted; it was no concern of mine. Some months later when looking over my checks I glanced at the one I had given him. The monetary amount I gave him was commensurate with the task he had performed, and would have made for a very nice outing for him, and his wife. The payee had been filled out to a local charity.

The night of the service, different people came and put various things on top of the coffin. We chose to have only an evening service. I placed my stuffed dog "Retread" on the coffin. Retread had been up at the hospital almost as much as Joshua. Retread was a stuffed dog with a Green Beret on his head and a Ranger tab sewn into his chest. Believe it or not, many of the guys in Special Forces and the Rangers have stuffed animals that we traveled with. I also had a Sesame Street blanket I went to the field with; a gift from my daughter when she was very young. My brother David placed his Special Forces coin on the coffin lid as well. Also placed was a wooden cross that Kristin had ordered. Again a shop teacher, Mr. Hawke, at Vo-Tech came through making a beautiful stand for it. Kristin also placed a plaque with Joshua's name and the meaning of the name. Additionally, she placed a small poem about how Joshua was more than a brother, but a friend as well. A small gold cross and a Star of David were placed over the wooden cross. His hockey team brought a little ball with the No. 12 on it and asked if they could put it on top of the coffin. We said that was absolutely a great thing to do. We still have the ball in our house. As far as the roller hockey games went, the woman in charge of the roller rink retired the number 12. The only person that will ever wear the No. 12 will be Dakota, my daughter's son. Eventually, I think it's really going to be nice if he ever gets into roller blading or hockey and wears Joshua's No. 12. Several people that knew him also either gave us notes to be placed in the coffin or laid them on top. All of those notes were placed in the coffin prior to Joshua being cremated. All of them were placed unopened and remained a private matter between Joshua and their authors. The cremation took place the next day with Joshua dressed in his hockey uniform, the notes, and the Green Beret I last wore while assigned to the 5$^{th}$ Special Forces Unit clutched in his left hand. All the other things that could not be sent with him, because of the material (i.e. metal), remain, till this day, under his picture at our house. The only thing returned was my brother David's Special Forces coin. I returned it to him and told him to keep it as a remembrance of Joshua and all the good they did each other.

Why was Joshua cremated? We decided that Joshua would be cremated partly because we really didn't know where to bury him. He was born in Grand Junction, Colorado. He had lived in North Carolina. He had lived in New Jersey. Nothing seemed appropriate. Pat was strongly against putting him in the ground. We also believe that Joshua would not have wanted to be placed in the ground, stuck in some old coffin. So the decision was made to cremate him and maybe take his ashes and place them under a tree and let the tree grow and it would be almost like a living memorial to him. As it turns out, his ashes were not dispersed from the funeral home. Pat and I thought about and discussed what to do with the ashes for about four months. Finally we decided there was no hurry and we preferred to leave them in our house for now. With that decision, we contacted the funeral home and purchased a really nice urn. The urn was engraved with a nice poem and has two crossed hockey sticks. His ashes are setting on a shelf in our house in New Jersey. At this point in time, my wife doubts that we will ever spread the ashes. If we ever did spread his ashes, my money is on planting them and a tree over at the Vo-Tech School in East Brunswick. Of all the places we visited, and of all the things we did, the Vo-Tech had the strongest impact on him. We even thought about spreading the ashes on the path leading from the Vo-Tech School to the mall because that was one of his favorite things, going over to the mall.

I believe it was also sometime before the service that we found out about Jamie's mom, Donna, going to the hospital to donate blood. She was upset when she found out Joshua had died and there was nothing she could do. Seeing her later, she actually felt bad and it was almost as if she felt it was her fault that things didn't work out for Joshua because of something she did or did not do. Well, it's totally not logical. On several occasions after Joshua's funeral, I bumped into Donna. She's a great gal. I don't know why but every time I see her, I feel the need to give her a warm hug and tell her how important she was. I think she'll always hold a special place in my heart. What's remarkable is that she doesn't see her role as being that significant. She couldn't have played a more important role if she had sought one out. Her feelings are a testament to her charity and compassion. I would ask God to bless her, but I already know that he does.

# CHAPTER XV

# The Service

I'm sure we violated all the rules on how to conduct a funeral service. The beginning of the evening was a little bit uneasy. Showing up early were my brothers, their families, and my parents. The casket was open at that point but viewing was limited to Pat, Kristin, Dr. Michaels, and me. We believed that was the way Joshua would have wanted it. The coffin was closed to all others. Jimmy was pretty emotional that evening. My mother was pretty emotional. I think my father had the most difficulty. He was sitting in the lobby of the funeral home and he just couldn't go into the room. Since we were a few minutes away from people arriving, I had to get my father to take his place for the service. Even though no one other than the four mentioned above saw the coffin open, I needed to make sure my father had a few moments of private time with Joshua. I had to go to the lobby and I looked at him, explaining to him that it was time. He responded, "His legs would not work." I tried to figure out some way of helping him. I looked him right in the eye, took his hand, and told him we needed to go now and pulled him to his feet. Together my dad and I walked to the back room and as we approached the coffin, he just couldn't take it anymore and his legs collapsed and my dad fell on the floor, pulling me with him. That caught everybody off guard. I've never seen him look so weak. My father is a very strong and powerful man. He was not at the height of his strength, for lack of a different way of wording it.

I asked my brother Jimmy to go get a chair and bring it over to the coffin. David and I picked my father up and put him back on his feet and assisted him to the chair. We then just let him sit there. He really looked old and sad sitting there, but at least he had a few minutes to say goodbye.

One really nice thing was that we had these little baseball cards made up with Joshua in his hockey uniform. When my wife had contacted the photographer that did the cards, she asked if there was any way to make a picture. He made one of these blown-up posters and they did it practically overnight. The photographer made it very reasonable, only charging us what the vendor charged him. His small act of kindness was, and always will be, appreciated. We took Joshua's picture down to the mall in Freehold and they framed it for us and put a nice little gold plaque on it. The whole production came out really nice and to this day the picture hangs in our living room. During the service, the picture remained propped up alongside the coffin. It was a nice touch since the casket was going to be closed during the ceremony. As the service went on, we were convinced that Joshua would have absolutely hated an open casket. There was some really nice flower arrangements that people had sent.

When people started coming in, we had chairs on both sides and an aisle in the middle and then the sitting area extended again in the back. The sitting area took on an "L" shape composed of the separate sitting areas. Pat made it her job to make everybody as comfortable as possible. As each person came in, she would talk to him or her and give them a really nice hug. We were standing approximately ten feet in front of the casket.

After they conversed with Pat, they would then approach the casket and take whatever time they needed.

I was standing next to Pat, just a short distance from the coffin. Some people I shook their hand, others I just said hi. Pat took it upon herself to make everybody feel at ease as much as you could at that kind of ceremony. It seemed like this went on quite a long time. Many, many people showed up. The one person I do remember talking to as if it happened yesterday was one of Joshua's doctors who made the comment she was glad she had listened to me and written the note taking Joshua out of gym. She said had she not written that note, it would have been very emotional for her. I think it reinforces what the doctors already knew: the doctors should listen to the parents because the parents know. Parents are always with the kids 24/7. I know the whole "note" incident convinced this one doctor that the best course of action was to listen to the parents and respond to the parents' requests whenever possible.

It was unbelievable to see that many people at a funeral. It seemed Joshua had a large impact on many people's lives. The entire building filled up to the point where people had to stand. By the time we were done, it was three hundred plus and Pat made sure she greeted everybody. After what seemed to be at least an hour to an hour and a half – I'm not sure how long it was – the pastor began the service. Joshua's cousin, Ashley Bell, sang a really beautiful song about love. Then it was my turn to talk. Before the service, the funeral folks had asked if somebody was going to say something. We just said no; just do the service and that would be the evening. Sitting there quietly, not saying anything about Joshua just didn't seem to be the appropriate thing to do. So I jotted a few notes down. I stood up and talked for awhile. One of the biggest regrets that I have is that we didn't tape this service because the service was beautiful. The pastor talked about Joshua's name, the fact that Joshua was a biblical character and his middle name was Jacob for his grandfather. His last name Laurie obviously because that's our surname. He talked about the impact that Joshua had on people. It was not an extremely strong religious service but it was obvious that the pastor put a great deal of time and effort into what he was going to say.

When it was my turn to speak, I talked a little bit about Joshua, his personality, and the things he did. I remember talking about the medical staff. Several of the doctors and nurses and other support personnel had shown up at the service. I remember making the comment that to choose a job working with dying children would truly be the hardest thing to do. I applauded them and everyone followed along. There were two things I forgot to talk about. The first thing I neglected to mention was that my Uncle Lou had recently died of leukemia. My Aunt Irene came up to me after the service and said that Uncle Lou would be up in Heaven waiting for Joshua. It was a nice thought. The second I didn't remember till later. I wish I had mentioned how nice all the TWA® folks were on our trip to Florida. In particular, a flight attendant named Joseph. It was soon after returning that Joshua relapsed and in all the turmoil I forgot to call Joseph and give a point of contact for the *Make A Wish Program®*. I truly hope if he ever sees this he understands. Of all the things we did, Joshua never did get his wish to be a voice in a Disney® animated film. But hell, he did like Hooters® and those cigars!

Ernie was there. Ernie didn't stay for the whole ceremony. Joshua's death took him pretty hard. I hope Ernie doesn't ever feel bad about leaving early. Ernie was there when he needed to be there, and for that we will always love him. He was there with Joshua playing Nintendo. He was there with Joshua going to the mall. He was there when Joshua was feeling bad. He was there when Joshua was feeling good. So we really thank God for Ernie. Jason was there too. Jason stayed for the ceremony. I remember acknowledging him in my little speech. Ernie and Jason - definitely two different kinds of folks. Ernie was a real straight-arrow kid. Jason, on the other hand, was a little more lively, a little more sneaky, and we're really glad to have Jason. If Joshua needed to be outrageous, we knew that he had somebody he could get outrageous with. Both Ernie and Jason had kept an eye on Joshua, and they could be counted on not to let him do anything stupid that would make his condition worse.

In finishing my speech, I had relayed the cigar on the parking deck story as well as a few others. I finished with Joshua, we love you and I will miss you. I'm sure the whole thing didn't go more than ten to twelve minutes. The pastor said a few more things and then there would be the final walk-by of the casket. Again, Pat took a moment with everybody as they left. It was amazing how much of an impact Joshua had on folks. By the time we got to the final walk-by of the casket, there wasn't a dry eye in the house. Everybody was pretty emotional. I'm sure people took solace in knowing it was okay to cry. Several of my brother's friends came by and they didn't know Joshua all that well but it didn't matter if you were six-foot-four and a two-hundred-and-ninety-pound bodybuilder or you were a little old lady; everybody cried with equal passion.

What was really nice was that when people came by whom we didn't know, they would tell a little bit about Joshua. Many of these strangers would share little, teeny, tiny stories in a matter of moments. I'm sure Pat is going to take the memories of those stories with her for the rest of her life. Known to us or strangers, all were welcome, and all were appreciated. By the end of the night, we were pretty worn out.

The funeral director came out after the service and said that the reception would be at my parents' house over in New Brunswick and they could pick up directions at the front entrance to the building. This process made it a lot easier for the folks to find my father's house. All were welcome who wanted to attend the after-service get-together. I always appreciated my parents opening up their home for this.

As we got ready to leave the funeral home, the lady in charge asked us what we would like to do with the flowers. We instructed her to do whatever you do with flowers after the service. She said that usually they take them to the local nursing homes and give them away. We said that was fine by us. She further commented on one of the very large flower arrangements. All the arrangements were beautiful. What made this one unique was the way the card was signed. What made it even more memorable was when the funeral director said that one of Joshua's friends even played a practical joke. I asked her what she meant and she showed me the card from the flowers and it was signed after a brief message with Avery, "Captain Sisko," Brooks. She said one of Joshua's friends had done this and she thought it was cute. I explained to her that the note and flowers came from a friend and his wife. Further that the signature was true, accurate, and a testament to a kind heart.

At my parents' house we had coffee and cookies. We kept it very simple. Most people didn't come. It was a very small group. I think maybe up to fifty people showed up at my parents' house, as opposed to the three hundred plus that were at his funeral. People came by and talked about Joshua and the various things. My brother's friend, Dave V., came down from Massachusetts. I hesitate to use the phrase, a typical military friendship, but David's friend Dave V. came down simply for the service and the next morning he had to go all the way back. That's just the kind of guy Dave V. is. If you called him and needed him to come, he would. My brother David had some other friends that had limited contact with Joshua. They also showed up and it was appreciated. A lot of friends from school came to the service but didn't come by the house. Some of his teachers came to the service. We appreciated all that came to the service and reception. I truly believe that Joshua knew they were there.

Within a matter of a couple of hours, everything ended and that was the end of the events for the entire evening. We found out from the funeral director that the next morning they would take Joshua in the casket over to the crematory and they would handle all that and then call us and tell us to pick up the ashes. Originally, as I said, we were going to have him cremated and have his ashes scattered. To facilitate, they were going to provide us with a little plastic-lined carton to hold Joshua's ashes. Four months later we changed our mind and got the gold urn I talked about earlier. My daughter went to the funeral home to pick up the ashes with her two friends Steve and Johnny. Once there, she purchased a pendant. The funeral home personnel then took the pendant and placed some of Joshua's ashes inside it. After placing the ashes inside, they then sealed the jewel piece with an epoxy. To this day, she wears it around her neck.

The day Joshua was cremated was rather interesting. People will tell you that they hear from the dead and they have premonitions and various things happen. I believe some of these things are just wishful thinking. For the most part, I don't understand how these things could happen. I guess I'm the typical, cynic, non-believer. At least I used to be.

Some of the things that happened on the day Joshua was cremated were unusual, to say the least. I'll start from the beginning so you will understand. When Joshua was about twelve years old, we had gone to Great Adventure®, which is down the road about a half an hour. We were walking around Great Adventure and we wound up in the arcade area. They have the frog game. This is where you take a hammer and you hit a little teeter-totter kind of thing, which launches the frog towards the lily pad. The idea is to have the frog land on the lily pad. Joshua wanted to play this silly game that cost two dollars for three frogs. I told him it was a joke, nobody won, it wasn't worth playing, and I tried every which way I could to dissuade him from doing this. Finally I thought to myself, this was one of his adventure days and he was entitled to do what he wanted to do. The whole purpose of having an adventure was to take one of the kids and let them do what they wanted to do, treat them as an equal. I found myself arguing over two dollars and in the scheme of things, two dollars was chump change. So I finally said, "Fine, here's the two dollars." I gave him the two dollars, reiterating to him that this was a joke because nobody ever wins these things and it's a total waste of money. Well, he put the first frog on the teeter-totter and he hit it with the hammer. The frog jumped through the air and landed on the lily pad, and they handed him a stuffed frog. Well, I told him it was my two dollars and I took the frog. He didn't really fight me on that. He was having fun showing me up, proving I was wrong and he was right. After all, he had indeed won the frog. That frog went in the left rear window of my car and has been there for years. Never moves. Never take it out. It's still there now. The day he was cremated, I had to go out to the car to get something. When I went out to the car and opened the back door, the frog fell out. The frog had never fallen out. It had never moved before. But the day he was cremated, the frog fell out. That gave me pause for something to think and dwell on.

Later that night, the light in the front yard, which had not been working for six months, chose to light up. Most people would say these are simple coincidences and have nothing to do with anything. I think I'm going to reserve judgment on that. If somebody had to hold me to an answer as to what I believed, I would actually go out on a limb and risk being called a nut by some people and say that both instances had something to do with Joshua. I believe Joshua is around me and when I do various things, I ask him for help. Particularly when I'm doing hypnosis shows. I believe he's present. Sometimes when I'm facing a particularly hard show, I'll ask him for help. One thing I have learned is that when you ask someone that has crossed over for help, be very clear about what you ask for. One of the funniest things that has ever happened to me, which was absolutely not funny at the time, was I had to work on one of the Carnival® Cruise Ships and the Cruise Director and I did not particularly get along. We had worked together on another boat where I had asked one of the social hosts how long the show would be. I don't know whether they were being sarcastic or silly or figured I should know, anyway but they told me to go an hour ten to an hour twenty minutes. So I ran the show for an hour thirteen minutes, said Good night and walked off stage. When you work on a cruise ship, whatever time they tell you they want, that's the time you give them. If they say they want a forty-nine minute show, in forty-nine minutes, you should be walking off the stage, this **time importance** is the same when you work casinos. If the casino entertainment staff wants a fifty-two minute show, you give them fifty-two minutes. No more, no less. Unbeknownst to me, the cruise director had wanted a forty-eight minute show, not an hour and thirteen minutes. I learned a very important lesson that day to always talk to the man in charge, and not one of the underlings.

When I showed up on this new boat, he was the Cruise Director and I knew things would not go well. So just before the show, I said to my son, Joshua, "I know you can hear me. I need these people to go out fast and deep." I went out and started my show, picked my subjects, had them sit in chairs, told them take a deep breath, close their eyes and go into deep, deep, deep hypnosis and they did. Twelve people went out. They went out in deep hypnosis and they sat there. No matter what I said, they didn't move. I told them they were hot, they had no reaction. I told them they were cold, they had no reaction. If you ever want to feel at a loss, be in front of fifteen hundred people with twelve subjects under hypnosis and no one moves or reacts. It doesn't make for a good show. I ended up stopping the show early by turning it into a lecture/demonstration. The same thing happened during the next show. I ended up doing a few very simple things and let some people take some pictures of people holding their hands up and putting their hands on top of their heads. It was a horrible, horrible show. Everybody in show business will tell you that sooner or later, you have to have a horrible show. Well, this was it. The Cruise Director was very gracious. He said, "These things happen." And we would go on from there. I didn't have a midnight show that night, so that evening was done.

When I returned home, I relayed what had happened to my wife and she said, "Well, what did you ask Joshua to do?" I expressed that I asked him to make them go out and go deep. Well, her response to me was, "that was exactly what he did, he made them go out, he made them go deep and you didn't tell him you needed them to do things." That was a very important lesson that night.

Whether you believe in communicating with someone who has crossed over or not, it really doesn't matter. All I knew was that I asked Joshua to let them go out and go out deep and that's exactly what happened in two shows back to back. Now the statistical significance of that happening at a random situation, I don't even want to begin to imagine. Well, lo and behold, the following week I had to go back to the same boat and of course I had the same Cruise Director. This time before the show, I looked in the mirror and said, "Look, Joshua, this guy does not like me. If he liked me at all, he really doesn't like me now because the two shows last week were horrible." Of course, this is a whole new set of passengers. So I looked in the mirror and said, "Joshua, I need them to go out, I need them to go deep but I need them to do stuff. This is a comedy show. We're here to make people laugh. If these people don't do something, I will look like a fool and I will not be asked to come back by this guy. I need them to do outrageous things. I need them to get silly. I need them to have fun. I just need to have something really, really wild here tonight. Understand? This is what I need. Out, deep, and silly."

When I got backstage, of course the Cruise Director was there and we shook hands and he asked me how I was doing. This concern for me was nothing more than being polite on his part and then he told me if things don't work out tonight, just end the show and we'll go on. Don't try to drag it out. I told him, we're not going to have that problem. "Every once in awhile I'll have a bad show. Last week we had a bad show. Tonight we'll be outrageous. Don't sweat the small stuff." He said fine, but then he reiterated that if things didn't go well, just end the show and get off the stage. I said, "Fine; no problem." I went on stage, talked to the audience for a few minutes, had a big group come up on stage, and from the big group picked my final 12. They sat in the chairs. I counted from ten down to one.

Almost immediately they all closed their eyes and got in a very relaxed position, and then I stood back and said when I count to two, take a deep breath and sit straight up in your chairs, eyes closed in deep, deep hypnosis. One, Two. When I did that, they all sat straight up in their chairs, sitting almost at an attention position, and then I went into my show. Typically I give them the experience of being warm and then cold and go on to other things. To say that these people acted as if they were professional hypnosis subjects would be an understatement. The show got outrageous. Everybody was very demonstrative. They were very outgoing. Their movements were exaggerated. When I told them they were hot, they immediately started sweating and fanning their faces. When I told them they were cold, they were literally climbing on top of each other using body heat to keep them warm. When they were given shrinking underwear, it was as if the underwear was crawling up around their ears. People were speaking what they thought was Japanese. People were thinking they were Martians from outer space. When I called for my hypnosis subjects to believe they were in an audition, they used body language and facial expressions to convince these invisible producers and directors to hire them. Their actions were spontaneous and believable. When they were vampires, they all had fangs and snarls and growls. Teeth were shining and showing. The show could not have been better if I scripted it and hired professional actors to play the parts. You would have thought they were plants in the audience, the way things worked out. As a final thing, I told everybody to take a deep breath and relax. I was getting ready to bring them up and have them go back to their chairs when I had a thought. So I took the microphone and put it behind me so the people could see that I did not intend for them or the entertainment staff to hear what I said. I told them that after they go back into the audience, when the Cruise Director says my last name, all the women would come and give him a warm, wonderful hug. Then I immediately brought the microphone back and went into my speech, "I'm going to count from one to five, and when I get to five, you'll open your eyes and get a warm and wonderful feeling, free of all stress and discomfort." I stated further that all the suggestions except the final one I gave you will be gone and you are to go about your evening and have a great time. Of course, nobody knew what that final one was and I'm sure there was some curiosity in the audience as well as by the Cruise Director. I then counted to five and they opened their eyes and they went back to their seats.

The way you end a show on a cruise ship is the same every time. You say on behalf of the Captain and Cruise Director and go on and on and give a little ten-second speech and then you say good night and walk off. The Cruise Director then walks out and says, "Ladies and gentlemen, let's give it up one more time for Jack Laurie" and you walk out and wave to them and you walk offstage and out the back. When he walked up on stage, I was in the front area. I had walked offstage towards the sound booth, which is actually down into the audience area.

The Cruise Director walks up on the stage and I had already told the cameraman to keep the camera on the Cruise Director and not to turn off the film. Later that night, they play the video on the ship's TV channel. Sure enough, as soon as I had exited the stage, the Cruise Director walks up on-stage and says, "Ladies and gentlemen, give it up for Jack Laurie." At that monument all the women immediately got up and ran on-stage and just gave this guy really wonderful, warm hugs. Just very nice people giving a wonderful, warm hug to another human being. Getting such a great set of hugs caught the Cruise Director off guard. He was in hog heaven. He thought that was a fantastic experience and a great way to end the show. The Cruise Director gave me a thumbs up and after that we actually got along quite well.

The whole experience taught me that when I ask for something, be very specific what I ask for. If you ask something of someone who has crossed over, you have to ask for exactly what you want. What I had asked for the previous week was for them to go out fast and deep, and that's what they did. This time I asked for them to go out fast and deep but they had to be silly and do things and respond to my voice and listen to my voice, and that's what they did. When I know I'm going to have a hard show, I'll ask Joshua to help me, but what I ask for is out fast, out deep, and doing stuff. So far, every time it has worked out very well.

## Other Happenings

One other time that I believe Joshua communicated to me - I hate to use the word "communicate" but one other time I felt that he was involved in the on-goings of what was taking place was when I saw the movie, *Seventh Day*. It was Arnold

Schwarzenegger's movie. I don't want to tell anybody the end of the movie because they may not have seen it and I'm sure somebody will rent it one of these days. At the end of the movie, Arnold Schwarzenegger, who was a father and husband, had an experience by which he was going to cross over. The radio in my Toyota Four Runner® doesn't work that well. I never worry about it because it's an extra car that we use when it snows. I have the volume turned off. As I was driving home, I was thinking that if I were ever to die, it would be a really neat thing that I would see my son again. At the same moment that I had that thought, the radio spiked. It gave out this loud burst of static. It was as if my son was telling me, "Dad, it will be great when you get here but let's not hurry the process." That was rather spooky. I didn't really explain the entire thought process that I was going through because it was only a fleeting thought, but I did express to my wife that it was a rather spooky thing to be thinking about crossing over and the radio would do that to me. Her response, as always, was that Joshua was communicating with me, and it's just not my time to go yet.

My wife has contacted a couple of individuals with regard to communicating with Joshua. I don't know as I believe the people that talk to her but I choose not to dismiss them. She deals with one lady from North Carolina. She is called the Angel Lady because she works with angels. They talk about Joshua once in awhile. This lady says that Joshua is around me whenever I travel. I don't know if he is or isn't. To that point I would not bet money on it, but my wife is convinced that Joshua is around whenever I travel. I like to think that he is. Well, maybe I don't accept it one hundred percent but I'm surely not going to go out of my way to dismiss it. In another conversation the Angel Lady asked Pat if had I started on the book yet. It seems that Joshua told the Angel Lady that I needed to write a book. My wife had never had any conversations with this lady about my writing this book and I found it rather interesting.

# CHAPTER XVI

# The Following Day It Starts

The days following the funeral were hard, particularly on me. Pat seems to have a very strong faith and I guess Kristin does too. Me, I guess I'm selfish. I was entitled to a son. I wanted my son and my son, was no longer with me. I'm sure whatever God had plans for, he needed one more angel to help him out, and that's why he chose Joshua.

The time it hit hardest was always in the morning. It was always hard but there's something about waking up and knowing he isn't here anymore. I think for at least the first two weeks after he died, I would wake up in the morning and start crying. There wasn't much I could do about it. My wife would wrap her arms around me and kind of rub my head and never really said anything. I guess I would cry for twenty to thirty minutes and then I would go on with my day. This particular morning cry went on for quite a while. Having him gone created such a hole in my heart I don't feel that it will ever totally heal. All the things my son and I shared would never happen again. Even if I shared these things with others, there would never be another Joshua. My son was gone and that's all there was to it.

I found that different things set me off. There's neither rhyme nor reason to it. There's some commonality to it, I guess.

Anytime I was watching a TV show or a movie where there's a loving relationship, it has an effect. It need not be a parent/child relationship. It may even be as simple as a scene where a husband and wife are in love, or brothers, or sisters, or friends. It has to do with the fact that there is an emotional bond. I actually become jealous and it manifests itself in tears. I think back to different events or moments and the emotions fill me up to the point of over flowing my being. I'd come to a red light, I take time to pause and reflect, and the next thing I know, I'm thinking about my son and I start crying. Talking about my child quite often makes me start to cry. It's already been three years since he died, and I still end up crying when I think about him. In the beginning, to write this book, I dictated into a recorder. I'm told the person typing the original draft had difficulty because quite often, the tapes indicated a stop point and then would start up again. It was obvious that at this moment of dictation, the circumstances were particularly hard to bear. Many incidents relayed on the tape and then subsequently placed on paper were very emotional to talk about. One night I was watching TV viewing an episode of *Star Trek Voyager*® where Seven of Nine® had mentored a Borg® child, of all things. To Seven of Nine, this Borg child was almost like her son. In the end, Seven of Nine had to stand by while he died, knowing there was nothing she could do but be there for him. Not letting him die alone consumed her. I bet I cried for thirty minutes when I watched that episode. I know some people will say that this is just science fiction and a TV show and it really didn't matter. It just hit home.

I try not to impose my feelings on other people and I think I've done a pretty good job of not doing that. One time I didn't hold my tongue was when I was coming back from one of the Carnival® Ships and I was passing through JFK Airport. The airport chose that night to lose my luggage. I was in the office in the airport where you fill out the claim form. There was a father there with three kids. He lost his three-hundred-dollar camera because somebody had stolen it out of his luggage. He was taking it out on the kids and he was screaming at them and threatening them. This was about two months after Joshua died. He was ranting and raving to the point that he was just getting ridiculous in his viciousness. I understood this because what he was doing, I saw myself doing the same thing years before. After listening to his ranting, I finally turned around and said, "Look, my son just died two months ago. I'd give anything to have him here. Your children have nothing to do with somebody stealing your camera. So why don't you lighten up?" I guess that got his attention because even though he didn't turn into a happy camper, he stopped threatening his children. This was the first time I had ever done anything like that, and most likely would be the last time.

One time I did impose my feelings and thoughts that was totally appropriate was when dealing with Guy. Guy is a family friend and a local police officer. Guy came to me with what he believed was an awful problem. He had been up to the hospital to the various children's wards. He knew of Joshua and had even been up to see him during his stays at the hospital. Guy's dilemma was that he needed to know how to handle dying children. He had remarked he had to keep leaving the children's ward area because he could not help but cry at the thought of the children that he was talking to were dying and there was nothing that he could do. He wanted to know how I handled it.

I first told him that you just do. I then told him that the crying was something that he had to handle. These kids are sick and crying is about you, not them. I told him it was okay to feel bad, and that he could cry all he wanted later. Now he needed to get up there and put in his mind that these kids needed a little joy, even if it was only for a few days. If he thought that he could provide a little joy, perhaps sunshine, even a little hope, then he should get his butt back up there and remember why he was there. Guy went back the next day and for years after that would make return trip after return trip. I know it still hurts him going back, and I know he still went back. You will hear more about this remarkable man later.

What I really get a kick out of is watching parents with their kids. It's a great thing that they have their children. It makes me quite jealous, actually. I wish that I still had my son. The grief gets easier as time goes on. Things still get to you, though. Ernie, Joshua's friend, getting his driving permit was a very emotional time because Joshua would have gotten his permit eight months after he died. Then you start thinking about all the times he'd want to borrow the car and you'd tell him no. This year would have been the year he graduated from high school. I feel sorry for myself not being able to see him walk across the stage to get his high school diploma.

Another aspect about treating your child's illness is that it soon becomes a way of life. Everything revolves around that. After Joshua died, we went to dinner at Olive Garden with my brother David and his wife. Now you might wonder what is so interesting about that. As we are sitting there, I realized and made the comment that it had been a little over four years since we had been out with another couple. Pat and I frequently went out to dinner, but always with just us. It was our way of taking a break away from all that was going on. Of course most of the conversations always revolved around the treatment of the day. It's a lot of fun, a nice change, going to dinner with them. As far as travel, after Joshua was diagnosed, we never both went out of town at the same time.

Still another thing that happens without any conscious thought is how we reference time and past events. Everything becomes "Oh, that happened before our son got sick." or "Oh, yes, I remember that, that was just after our son died." It's not that you mean to reference everything that way. Maybe some day we will look at things as, "Oh yeah, that happened after the Mets® (hoping) won the World Series®." Time will tell.

In the Army we have a saying, "There is always one person who does not get the word." Well, that was Lou. Lou had limited contact with Joshua. His contact was just through me. Lou is a real estate agent. Lou's a pretty good guy. Always dressed to the hilt. Looks really good, long hair and all. I felt bad for Lou because Lou used to always ask about Joshua and then after Joshua died, I hadn't seen Lou for quite some time and like I said, there's always that one person who doesn't get the word. About sixteen months after Joshua died, I popped into the real estate office just to say "Hi." My business requires that I work with a lot of Realtors®. For some reason, our paths hadn't crossed yet. I walked in and as soon as he saw me, he said, "Hi, how are you doing?" He shook my hand. While he was shaking my hand, he had this big smile on his face and he asked how Joshua was. Well, that was an awkward moment. I had to tell him that things hadn't worked out for Joshua. He was instantly upset. Not only was he upset because Joshua died but I think he was upset that I would perceive his statement to be very callous in asking me how he was. His demeanor, his body language, everything, showed me that this was a very awkward moment for him. It needn't have been but I understood it and tried as best as I could to put him at ease and explain to him that yes, Joshua had died and it was not that big a deal that he didn't know. I thanked him for asking. Some of the people that Joshua had an effect on were family and close friends, others just a momentary thing where their paths crossed briefly and would never cross again. Even those people that he didn't interact with often still feel Joshua's touch.

One thing I did find out after the funeral was that Jason made a videotape, and on the videotape, they were talking about Joshua kissing a girl. This tape was a way that Joshua's friends could say "Hi!" We hadn't seen the tapes before because Joshua asked us not to look at them. I don't know why that was important but it was really a great thing that Joshua had experienced his first kiss. More interesting than that, jokingly, my wife asked me, "What if he wanted something else from a girl?"

To which I responded, "Well, he never asked to experience sex, but had he asked for the services of a very nice woman, I probably would arrange it." I know that probably irritates some people but my mindset was that in case things didn't work out, I was going to let him experience anything he wanted to. But, he didn't ask and I didn't offer.

Vacations are hard. When I go on vacations, I see parents enjoying their kids. I watch parents playing with their children, showing them things, and teaching them the things they need to know. At times, it's very upsetting. Joshua would say things to my wife that he wouldn't say to me. He would tell his mom that if he died, she would still have Koty. My wife's response was always, "Koty was Kristin's child and we would never be able to replace you. Don't give up. You have a lot to live for." No matter how many times she'd say that, his response was always, if I die, you still have Koty. I don't know why he never said that to me. He never did, but he would hammer that home to my wife all the time.

I'm really happy for Koty because now Koty is almost five years old and coming into his own. Recently I started to take Koty on adventures. Adventures are nothing more than a fun trip. It could last part of a day, a whole day, or even a couple of days. It's something that we do out of the ordinary. On Koty's first adventure, I took him to McDonald's® playground and we played until he was done playing. I think we spent an hour and forty-five minutes to two hours at the playground. He got to play on all the slides and the tunnels and he even got to play in the little plastic ball pit. There was no pretense that we had to hurry up to go on to do things. We were just going to let things take their course. We were going to take our time and have FUN.

After he got done playing, I took him down to the gentleman that designed the tattoo I carry on my upper arm symbolizing Joshua. I asked Tommy, the tattoo artist, if he wouldn't mind working on Koty. Of course Tommy immediately agreed. So I let Koty pick out his first tattoo and he picked out a big snow tiger. The tattoo was about five by five inches. Tommy made a tattoo stencil with a device that looks almost like a photocopier. The stencil is a blue ink background that they trace the tattoo outline onto your skin. The true talent comes with coloring it in and refining it. So Tommy had him raise his shirt and he put the little roll-on stuff on so the tattoo sticks. Koty was a little apprehensive. He thought Tommy was going to take out the machine and start in with the needles. I explained to Koty that this was not going to hurt him and he picked up his shirt and Tommy put this big snow tiger on his chest. Tommy then dried the stencil ink and that was as far as the process went. Koty was extremely proud of his tattoo and he showed it to his mom, my wife, the waitress in the diner, and he showed it to the kids on the street. Come to think of it, I don't think there's a person in New Jersey that has not seen his first tattoo. It lasted about two weeks and he thought that was the greatest thing since peanut butter.

With regard to the tattoo I have on my upper left arm, I'll try to describe it the best I can. It is a large Celtic cross, and interwoven at the top is a Star of David. Across the top piece is tattooed the word "SON," and down the centerpiece is the name "JOSHUA." At the base, the cross has the appearance of being buried and is surrounded by four rocks, two large rocks representing Pat and I and two smaller ones representing Kristin and Koty. A crack in the cross with a tear running out finishes the design. The colors are mostly yellows and greens.

Koty's second adventure was back at the McDonald's playground for an hour or so and then we went to the aquarium and I let him run loose there. By that I mean he was always next to me but whichever way he wanted to go and whichever exhibit he wanted to see is what we went and experienced. It's always a great feeling taking him on these adventures because now it's his time. Kristin gets a little bit irritated because she doesn't get to go, but it irritates her in a funny way. She gives me a hard time asking about her next adventure. I tell her that her time has come and gone and now it's Koty's turn. I know I need to keep taking her away occasionally because she still needs a daddy and I still need her. Awhile back, we went on our latest adventure. Kristin and I went to San Francisco. Kristin's adventures will not be as glorious as they used to be. I doubt there's ever going to be another Disney World, ski trip or para-gliding experience. But I'm looking forward to quiet dinners. Maybe we can go into New York City occasionally.

One thing I did experience that was a dilemma of sorts while on a recent trip with Kristin. I hate to fly. Yes, I know I fly all the time. That doesn't change the fact that I hate to fly. Actually it's not the flying per se but the landing. My brother David is just the opposite; he hates the taking off. As we start to descend to land, I get nervous. To stay calm, I say to myself, "If we crash, I will cross over with Joshua. If we arrive safely, I will live for Kristin." That is what works for me along with some breathing exercises. The only problem is, I started to say my special phrase to myself when we were about to land and I realized that Kristin was on the plane with me. Oh, well, back to just the deep breathing exercises that I know.

What I'm really looking forward to is taking Koty and his new sister Iliana on adventures. While Koty is almost five, Iliana is just over one year old. Before you know it, Iliana will be old enough to go on her own adventures; just the two of us. I've already been told that I can take Koty to Disney World. I'll have to wait a couple of years till he's bigger. I'm looking forward to it. I'm assuming that's going to be a very emotional experience. Emotional experiences are all right. I know if it gets too hard on me, I've got family that will support me and take care of me.

One of the most indelible experiences/events that happened after Joshua died was a late night call I received from my brother Jimmy. I answered the phone and he was crying. I said, "Who is this and he just responded, "me." "What's up" is all I said. He then proceeded to tell me that he and Lorna were proud of me and Pat and the way we handled everything over the last few years. That's all he said and then he said we would talk later and hung up the phone after I said, "Thanks." I have a remarkable family. The whole time Joshua was sick, right up to the end, no one interfered. Not one member stuck their nose into our business or offered suggestions as to how we might do things differently. That leaving us to do what we felt we had to do was much appreciated, and will always be remembered. One other thing that will also hold a special appreciation for us was the naming of Jimmy's new son; James Joshua Laurie.

# CHAPTER XVII

# Feelings, Bears, and a Song

I don't know why it is but it seems I'm the closest to Joshua when I'm traveling. This closeness is particularly strong if my travels involve working or vacationing on a boat. Boats are a nice vacation. You go on a cruise ship, you unpack, and you can follow their schedule or you can just hang out in your room or out on deck. One tradition I seem to have started is that the last night that I'm on a boat, that's Joshua's night with me. I get my cigar and I go up on deck and just sit there by myself. I call it Joshua time. Some people understand it. Some people don't. Recently Guy and I went on the cruise. When you go on a cruise ship, people tend to start hanging out in groups. We got involved with this one particular group. The last night of the cruise, I told Guy that I would be going off by myself later that night to be with Joshua. Guy knew Joshua as my son and also from his hospital visits. He was around when Joshua was sick and he was at the funeral. He knew that this was a serious time for me and he just left me alone.

I went up on deck and later on I found out that a couple of people were asking where I was. Guy told them I was up on deck smoking a cigar with my son, which was the way I always referred to it. Their response was that they weren't aware that my son had been on the cruise with us. He explained that Joshua had been sick and he died and this was my time with him. Some of the people said they would come up on deck and keep me company because I probably shouldn't be alone. Guy told them to just butt out; I was up there and he told them to stay away from me. What was really interesting is that I found out one of the women in the group remarked that obviously I hadn't settled this issue, and she should go up there and help me, as she said, come to terms with Joshua's death. Guy told her that I absolutely had come to terms with Joshua's death and she could keep herself right where she was and there was no way he was going to let her interfere with my Joshua time. At the time Guy's actions were very much appreciated. It is always the small kindnesses offered by a person that tends to stick out in my mind. I wonder why that is?

Sometimes people will say that if you're still emotional about the passing of someone, that means that you have not come to terms with their death. I know it's a cold, callous opinion on my part, but obviously, they have no idea of what they're talking about. I came to terms with the death of my son when I held him and sent him to God. I understood he was dead and I understood he wasn't coming back. I also understand that I believe he communicates with me. I understand that he's around me. I understand that certain things will always have an impact on me. I've come to terms with the fact that my son is dead. That doesn't change the fact that I miss him dearly, and at times, it's extremely emotional and hard to be without him.

Recently I had the experience of buying a new motorcycle. It's really interesting the way I wound up with that motorcycle. A while back I purchased my brother's Harley-Davidson® and it seemed that at this time in my life, I'm supposed to have a new Harley-Davidson. I'm sure it's strictly ego. It's a sign of success. It's a sign of being macho. It's a sign of, "Look, I've got a Harley-Davidson. I have a loud, thundering motorcycle and don't you wish you had one?" I really didn't need a new bike. I had thought about buying a new bike but with the amount of money that they cost, it just didn't make any sense. Then I came out of my office one day and I saw a guy I knew. I asked him why he was in the parking lot of my office building. He explained to me that his wife was seeing the doctor upstairs. No sooner after we started to chat, his wife joined us. She relayed to us that the doctor expressed to her that he would like to put her in the hospital for a day just to check a few things. Her response to that was she was a nurse and she would take care of it and it wasn't that big a deal. That was on a Wednesday. Friday afternoon they took her to the hospital. She ended up in Intensive Care with liver failure. We thought we were going to lose her. As luck would have it, they performed a liver transplant on her Sunday afternoon. Her recovery was amazingly rapid. She's still with us, thank God, and leading a very normal, healthy life. Well, when that happened, I said, well, you know, I could be dead tomorrow. So I went down to the Harley-Davidson dealer and I bought a new Harley-Davidson.

Now you might be asking why I am expressing this story to you. The salesman who I bought the Harley-Davidson from was the son of the owner of the store. I didn't know that when I was talking to him and negotiating the price of the bike. I found out who his father was more towards the end of the deal. When we closed the deal, I had the opportunity to talk to the owner at which time I relayed to him, "I didn't realize that was your son." He said, "Yes." He looked at me puzzled, obviously wondering why I was getting teary-eyed and glassy-eyed over the purchase of a motorcycle. I explained to him that I was extremely jealous. I had hoped to work with my son in my hypnosis business, but it was not to be; he had died the year prior. I told him it was really, really nice to see his son working with him. He thanked me and he understood the importance of it.

I think everybody ends up thinking that eventually they'll pass their business, or their equity, money, cars, or whatever, on to their children when they die. It's hard sometimes to face the fact that the child has already died. I think the expression is, "parents should not outlive their children." I believe that saying to be true, having a child die before the parents die, really, really sucks.

I could still work with my daughter; not! As much as I love my daughter, we don't work well together. She's very strong-willed. I'm very strong-willed. Some families are really good at playing together but not working together. Kristin and I do not work well together. We have a great time at everything else, but work, well, I guess that's life. Who knows, maybe in the years to come, if I'm still in the same business, Koty will start working with me. Maybe, just maybe, I'll have a chance to show him all about hypnosis.

For everything that we experience that is bad, I try to remember that others can have it worse. I recently did a hypnosis show in Texas for a high school. I started to talk to one of the chaperones and he asked if I had any kids, so I said yes and told him briefly about Joshua. He understood, having lost his son six years earlier. When I asked how it happened, he told me the story of his son going out for the day with some friends and on their way home, less than a mile away from the house, at a four-way intersection, his son's car was hit and he was killed. He saw his son leave that morning and a police officer was the last thing he saw that night. I had twenty-one months to play with, learn from, and enjoy the company of my son after we knew he might not make it. For that short time, I will always be grateful. Pat tells me that in the end, I had become Joshua's best friend, his pal, and his confidant. I couldn't have asked for a greater gift from a son.

As for the Rolex® watch I always wanted. The one Joshua had picked out the last night we went out on the town is worn on my left wrist. After Joshua died I sold my sailboat and added the funds to the money I had saved. I purchased the watch at Fords Jewelers® in Fords, New Jersey. What makes the watch even more special is the engraving I had them add to the back of the watch; his birthday, his name "Joshua," and the date of his death.

## J.J.'s Bears

In an effort to keep Joshua's memory alive, Kristin enlisted the aid of his school. Kristin explained to the students and teachers that she had a great idea to give bears to the kids in the hospital where Joshua spent much of his time. J.J.'s Bears was born. The reason bears were chosen was because that was an important request of Joshua to his sister. He wanted a nice, soft teddy bear. As with any request he made of his sister, this too, she delivered on, one soft cuddly teddy bear, which he loved. The Vo-Tech School immediately kicked in to help. One section of the school helped to construct a wagon, another group the handle. The next step in building this wagon of love was to have Joshua's grandfather paint the wagon red. Kristin took the wagon back to the Vo-Tech school for a custom-lettering job. Others at the school donated and collected bears. When all was said and done, we had a beautiful wagon filled to the brim with teddy bears and love. The teddy bears were distributed to the children in both the cancer clinic and up on the various children's wards. We continue to receive donated bears and distribute them. Many bears come from people who knew Joshua. Other bears come from hosts of my hypnosis shows and groups that sponsored various fundraisers that I worked. One thing that seems to be interesting is that when a group cannot afford my fee for a show I will tell them just to have folks bring in bears. This audience participation, instead of paying me my fee, tends to work very well for J.J.'s BEARS. If you add up the value of the bears, it usually exceeds the cost of what the show would have been; go figure. Rest assured no donated bear ever went hungry or had to be turned out into the cold. If you would like to send a bear to J.J.'s Bears, send them to Endeavors-J.J.s Bears, P.O. Box 922, Dayton, NJ 08810. For Bears arriving via UPS®, FedEx®, etc., contact Endeavors at 732-329-8570 for shipping information. The bears must be "**NEW.**" The children that the bears are given to usually have a compromised immune system, and it would be unsafe to give them a used bear, no matter how much that bear has been loved.

## One Last Thought

Wonders never cease. Just when you think that maybe things are not as they seem something happens. It's been several years since the death of Joshua. I wonder as I read my own writings if I may be seeing the things that I want to see when it comes to Joshua's presence.

Last night I brought home a new car. Nothing fancy, just a Honda Accord® with a few options and a navigation system. One of the options was a satellite radio. I always wanted a satellite radio, and well, now I have one. So, I'm in the driveway trying to get the darn thing programmed when Kristin comes out and jumps into the passenger side of the vehicle. I have to add here that Kristin's favorite singer is Dolly Parton.

So we are sitting there trying to get the radio programmed, over 100 channels I might add, when she says we should see if it works. So we pick channel 10, no particular reason, and not knowing what type of music that channel will play. We set the radio accordingly. Of all the songs in the world, of all the singers in the world, of all the music that could come from this new toy we sit there in awe as the car fills with music for the first time from the many speakers. We look at each other as we recognize the voice of Dolly Parton singing Barry Sadler's *Ballad of the Green Berets*. I sometimes question if God is around me, but I know Joshua is.

As a side note to all this communicating with someone who has passed. In my own way I have found a way to talk to Joshua when I want to. Now this may sound silly, but some years ago I heard an American Indian flute being played for the first time. When I heard the flute I felt like it was talking to me; silly I know. Well anyway, I went and bought a few and now when I feel the need to talk with Joshua I play them. Mind you I'm not very good, but well, it works for me.

# CHAPTER XVIII

# The Letter

Oh, as for my hair, well, it has been a while now and ever since that last cut, I haven't cut it yet except for a little part in front so I can see. Recently a little boy, the son of a lady I met, asked me why I looked like a girl. So I sent him a little letter via his mom and told her if she thought that it was appropriate to give it to him now or some time in the future.

Dear Big Guy,

I heard you say "That guy has long hair like a girl." You know what, I do. But the most interesting thing is that I have long hair because of love. Now you might ask how could long hair and love go together. So let me tell you a story.

My name is Jack and I had a son named Joshua. Joshua was a lot like you. He was smart and had dark hair. One day when Joshua was 10 years old, I asked him to get a hair cut. Joshua didn't think that was a good idea. Do you know when your mom and dad think something is a good idea, but you don't? Sometimes it's over when to go to bed, or what to eat, like peas and carrots. Well, sometimes it is over things like hair. Joshua and I had a lot to say to each other about his hair. I tried to think of ways to get him to understand my side, the way I thought. He tried to get me to see the way he thought. Soon it became clear that we had to try something different; but how to do that?

I came up with an answer. I told him that if he wanted to grow his hair, I would grow mine. He thought that was funny. I thought it was funny too. So we started to grow our hair. It grew, and it grew, and it grew. Pretty soon my hair was all the way down to my belt. I had to put rubber bands in it to keep it out of my face, or I could not see to read or watch TV. Joshua thought all this was rather funny. This went on for three years. Imagine having three birthdays and not ever cutting your hair!

When Joshua was 13 years old, he kinda got sick. This was not the kind of sick that you get when you have a runny nose or get a cough. This was the kind of sick that makes mommies and daddies feel scared. He had a thing called leukemia. When you get this, you have to take very strong medicine. One of the medicines that Joshua took was so strong that it made his hair go away. This made Joshua sad. He thought that if he didn't have hair that he would look funny. Looking funny is no fun. Of course mommies and daddies try to make their kids feel good, so I told Joshua that he looked okay without hair. He said that it was easy for me to say that, because I had hair. He then said that is what all daddies say. That night I thought about what he said and I told his mommy that we would show Joshua that not having hair could be just as good as having hair. So I went to a friend of mine and he cut off my hair. Now I looked just like Joshua; no hair. When Joshua saw me without hair, he started to laugh. When Joshua's friends saw me without hair, they laughed too. I guess if you don't have hair, it can look funny.

Joshua and I had no hair for a long, long time. It was over a year before he started to have hair again. When he started to have hair again, so did I. After all, if he was going to grow hair, I would too. Pretty soon we each had HAIR. Our hair was almost as long as the little toe on a little boy's foot. Then one day Joshua had to go back to the doctor's office, where he found out some sad news. The medicine was not working anymore. So to try to make him well, they gave him some even stronger medicine. Guess what? He lost his hair again in just two days. So that night I thought, since he doesn't have hair, I guess I won't have hair. So I cut it off again so that we could be the same. When Joshua saw that I did not have hair, he smiled.

After a few days, Joshua was not feeling well. I think it was then that God asked Joshua if he could help him. I think God needed an angel that understood that little kids sometimes get scared when they get really sick. So, in his own way, Joshua asked his daddy, mommy, and sister if it would be okay if he went to help God understand how kids feel when they get really sick and scared. Now God has an angel that understands when kids are scared and don't always understand the things that go on around them.

After Joshua went to help God, I knew that he would let his hair grow again. So if he was going to let his hair grow, well, gee whiz, so would I. Ever since Joshua went to help God, I have not cut my hair. So that's why my hair is like it is. It is kinda like when your mommy and daddy put your really neat pictures on the refrigerator to show everyone. They put all those beautiful things out so people can see them because they are proud of you, and they want everyone to know all the wonderful things that you can do. See, parents do stuff like that because they love you. Mommies and daddies tell everyone about you for the same reason. Mommies and daddies are just that way. And do you want to know a secret? Another reason that they put all your pictures on the refrigerator is because whenever they see them, it reminds them of how beautiful and important you are to them. The reason my hair is long is for the same reason. My hair reminds me of Joshua and how beautiful and important he is.

Well, that's my story. That's why I have long hair like a girl. Maybe someday I will cut it. You never know. ☺

## THE END

# A SPECIAL THANKS

This last page is needed for all the great folks who aren't in my story. See, this is just that: my story. There were many others involved in Joshua's journey. Pat had support from family and friends, as did Kristin. I am sending a warm hug to all the wonderful people who touched my life and the lives of my family.

To Casey Noon, Annie Oakley, and Akash P. Patel who spent hours going over this book line by line so that Joshua's story could be as good as it could be, a special thanks. A big smile to Diane Noon, who helped create a great title. Add to this, a special acknowledgment to Charlotte Staake, John Fludas, and Carol Mulligan for the final edits. Also a warm thanks to those who offered to read the drafts but found them too emotional to read in their entirety just yet. To Lou Stalsworth who showed me the way to start this project in the first place. Lastly, to my family, friends, and especially my wife and daughter, a special thanks for just being you.

Any questions, comments, or observations
may be e-mailed to:
**Jackjlaurie@aol.com**

We welcome all visitors to our web sites at:
**www.canceranoceanoftears.com**
and
**www.jacklaurie.com**

# ABOUT THE AUTHOR

# JACK J. LAURIE

Jack J. Laurie has a varied military and business background. On the business side Jack Laurie owned one of the largest radon labs in the State of New Jersey from 1988 to 2001. In 2001 Jack Laurie merged with another company to allow for more time in managing the hypnosis/speaking side of his life. He remains as a radon consultant to this day.

As the owner and founder of the Hypnosis Center (South Brunswick, NJ), Jack J. Laurie received his first formal training in hypnosis in 1988 while attending the Harte Institute located in New York City. Jack Laurie holds a Bachelor's degree in Business Management from Mesa College of Grand Junction, Colorado. In addition he earned two Masters degrees. His first Masters, an M.A. in Human Resource Development came from Webster University in Saint Louis, Missouri. His second masters, an M.S.A. in Health Services came from Central Michigan University of Mount Pleasant, Michigan.

Jack J. Laurie is a former US Army Green Beret who holds the distinction of also being Ranger qualified. His assignments have included the 5th Special Forces Group, as well as the 7th Group, 10th Group, Special Operations Command (SOCOM), Special Operations Task Force Europe (SOTFE), and United States Army's Institute for Military Assistance (USAIMA).

In 1983 Jack Laurie was sent as one of two advisors to Korea with SEAL Team I to instruct the Navy in Isolation Security Operations.

Since 1994 Jack J. Laurie has become one of the most sought after speakers, trainers, and entertainers in the United States. Many of Jack Laurie's speaking engagements are related to subjects from business management, salesmanship utilizing Neuro Linguistic Programming (NLP) techniques, stress reduction, motivation, and expressing to families that they are not alone when a terrible loss is experienced. Joshua's story has defined his life in ways that he would have never imagined.

If you would like to seek out Jack J. Laurie
to speak as a keynote, guest lecturer, or need assistance
with a fundraiser feel free to contact him at:

**732-329-8570**

To write:

**Endeavors**
**Attention: Jack J. Laurie**
**P.O. Box 922**
**Dayton, New Jersey 08810**

E-mail should be sent to:

**Jackjlaurie@aol.com**
Enter: Comment-Ocean of Tears
on the subject line; please.

Visit the website at:

**www.jacklaurie.com**

# QUICK ORDER FORM

## CANCER: An Ocean of Tears

**Fax:** (732) 274-0260 (send this form or a copy of this form)

**Call:** (732) 329-8570 (inside NJ)
(800) 872-7236 (outside NJ – orders only)

**Web:** www.canceranoceanoftears.com

**Write:** Endeavors
Attn: Cancer – Jack Laurie
P.O. Box 922, Dayton, New Jersey  08810

❑ Please send me _____ copies of *CANCER: An Ocean of Tears*
at $14.95 each, plus shipping and handling.

Name: _____  Date: _____

Address: _____

City: _____  State: _____  Zip: _____

Phone: _____  Email: _____

---

**Sales tax:** Please add 6% for products shipped to New Jersey addresses.

**Shipping: US:** $4 for the first book and $3 for each additional book.

**International:** Based on ship-to location and current rates; please call
for exact amounts.

---

**Payment type:** ❑ Check/Money Order   Make checks and money orders payable to "Endeavors."

❑ Credit Card   ❑ Visa   ❑ Mastercard

Credit card #: _____

Name on card: _____  exp date: _____

Signature: _____

Credit Card Verification Number: _____

The Verification Number is the last group of numbers located on
the signature strip on the back of your credit card.

1234 567
Verification Number = last group of numbers